ECHO OF LOVE

ECHO OF LOVE

•

Mary Hagen

AVALON BOOKS
NEW YORK

Published by Thomas Bouregy & Co., Inc.
160 Madison Avenue, New York, NY 10016

Library of Congress Cataloging-in-Publication Data

Hagen, Mary (Mary Hirsig)
Echo of love / Mary Hagen.
p. cm.
ISBN 978-0-8034-9995-9
1. Single mothers—Fiction.   I. Title.
PS3608.A37E28 2010
813'.6—dc22
2009024251

PRINTED IN THE UNITED STATES OF AMERICA
ON ACID-FREE PAPER
BY HADDON CRAFTSMEN, BLOOMSBURG, PENNSYLVANIA

Chapter One

There was nothing unusual about the day, no electricity reverberating, no anxious tension tagging at Mori Jordan, nothing to suggest that her beginning-to-go-smoothly life was about to become complicated. That is until he pulled his fancy rig into her yard. Frowning, Mori leaned over the top railing of the corral and watched the blue Dodge 250 pickup with matching horse trailer pull to an abrupt stop. Now who is that?

He unfolded his tall frame from the driver's seat and stepped out in a man-with-a-mission style. His expensive suit, dazzling white shirt, and stylish tie belied his mission as he unloaded a frisky, young chestnut Morgan mare. Securing the halter onto her proud head, he eased his wide hand over her back and led the mare toward Mori. Except for the mare, his manner of dress and good looks reminded her of Frank, the ex-husband she was glad to be rid of.

Watching the man and horse, Mori almost let out a whistle. The man was a hunk, far more handsome than Frank and bigger too. In fact the hunk and the Morgan with her shining dark coat were a perfect pair. Curious about the man who walked toward the corral, Mori headed for the gate to open it. The jangle of her cell phone interrupted her intent, and she reluctantly took the call.

The sound of Cecile's voice, her partner at Riding Farm, softened her irritation. Her message further piqued Mori's curiosity. So the man who had driven into her life without warning was Mark Larson, *the* Mark Larson who had crossed her path those many years ago. And he wanted her to train his mare. *If that wasn't irony.* Cecile had hoped to be there when Larson arrived. Well, she hadn't made it, and Mori was on her own with the well-known lawyer.

Mori stuck her phone in her pocket and pushed open the gate, only to face "the hunk," who seemed even taller close up.

"Hi," Mark Larson said, as he extended his hand. "Cecile probably told you I'd be bringing my filly. Your partner speaks highly of you and said you'd be the best one to work with her since my schedule keeps me from doing it myself." He paused. "I doubt that you remember me."

"Cecile just called to let me know you were coming," Mori said, meeting his hand with hers.

She remembered him. His name registered the minute she had heard it. He looked different from the man she had known fourteen years earlier. She had not liked him. She measured him with a quick glance.

"I'm earlier than I thought I'd be," Mark said with a smile. "I hope it's not inconvenient."

"Not at all," Mori said as she circled the mare, examining her features. She ran her hand down the filly's leg, feeling the carpus and metacarpus bones. Mori's judgment rated the horse as sound and workable. Her judgment about the owner of the horse, the well-known bachelor in nearby Fort John, Colorado, wasn't so positive.

Larson and she had been in a horse show together when she was sixteen and he was in law school. He had looked down his well-formed nose and had spoken in a condescending tone, "You don't belong in this competition. You're too young to handle the mare you're riding. You should bow out before you embarrass yourself."

Mori had straightened her back, pushed her hair aside, and proved him wrong.

She no longer was intimidated. She stood her ground in the dusty driveway, fixing her gaze directly into Mark's eyes. "Her bone structure seems sound. What have you got in mind concerning the mare's future?"

Mark drew his eyebrows together for a second. "I'm not certain. She's green, hasn't had much attention. I like to ride Western, but don't want to put her under a saddle until she's ready, a bit older." He squinted and put his hand over his forehead to cut the brightness of the sun. "You're the expert. I'll leave it up to you."

The tension relaxed in Mori's neck as she said, "She's a fine animal. What's her name?"

"Sunny Day." His hand skimmed along the sheen of the horse's neck. "I can't wait to see how she comes along. I'd like to work with her too, whenever I can."

The pride in his voice and gentleness of his touch caught Mori up short. For a moment Mori made no comment, but took a deep breath. If Mark David Larson III became one of her clients and she did a good job, it would bring her business. That she could use! More than anything, Mori wanted to pay off her mortgage and make her horse business a success so that she could provide Emily with a secure home.

Mori glanced at his pickup and horse trailer. It smacked of wealth. Very few breeders could afford such a luxury rig. There was more to see, however. Why hadn't she noticed the occupant in the passenger side? Maybe the sun's reflection. She certainly saw her now, using every bit of grace to maneuver herself from the truck. There was no mistaking the beautiful socialite, Shawna Queensly. Mori had read about Mark and Shawna in the newspaper. They were together at most functions worthy of mention in the city paper.

Ignoring the woman leaning against the truck, Mori lifted her chin ever so slightly and turned her attention back to Mark. "I'd like to train Sunny Day." Cupping her hand around the soft velvet of Sunny Day's muzzle, she looked up into her large, prominent eyes and said, "Looks like we're going to be partners, Sunny Day."

Mori liked the strength of the head of the Morgan breed, the set of the ears, and the nice curve of the back. Mori noticed she had no white markings, not even on her face. Continuing to explore Sunny Day for any flaws, Mori addressed Mark, "I'll need a health certification from your vet. Don't want to bring any diseases to our horses."

"I gave them to Cecile when I discussed boarding and training fees with her at the chamber luncheon. Luckily, I had them with me. I've only had her a short time."

"Fair enough," Mori said.

Mark handed her Sunny's reins and that was that. He was entrusting the care and training of this beautiful animal to her. Nothing but good could happen to Sunny at Riding Farm.

That done, Mark's manner and voice were businesslike. I have three more horses I need to board. They'll need some work too. Would like to work them myself when time permits, but can't always drive the twenty-five miles to my ranch." He paused. "That's if you have time and room."

Mori rubbed her grimy palm over her jeans before she took the hand Mark offered. Looking into his smiling face with the gray eyes, she read friendliness.

"I'll check with you in a few days to see how it's going."

"Sounds good. I'll keep you informed about Sunny's

progress, what I'm doing. You can tell me if I'm on the right track, if it's what you had in mind."

"I'm sure this will work out for both of us. Unfortunately, I've got to get back to work." He headed for his truck, then turned, "Cecile has my phone number. If you need anything just call."

Mori watched him walk to his vehicle, the 'I'm sure this will work out for both of us,' ringing in her ears. He had lost none of his muscular athletic build she remembered from the horse show. Not like Frank. He'd grown flabby in the years she'd been married to him. Mori gave a sigh of intense relief, glad that phase of her life had ended, and then pondered the exchange between Mark and Shawna.

"Ready, Shawna?" she heard Mark call.

"Of course. That horse of yours gets more attention than I do," she said petulantly.

Mark opened the door to his truck and helped Shawna step in. She kissed him lightly.

Did Mark draw away from the kiss? Strange.

Mori compared her grubby jeans to Shawna's stunning blue suit and chic straw hat with the blue polka dot band that matched her blue and white silk blouse. The blue and white pumps made her almost as tall as Mark who, Mori guessed, was well over six feet tall.

"Back to work," Mori heard Mark say as he entered the truck.

"Humph," Mori said under her breath. "Hardly the

appropriate clothes for a horse delivery, even if they did come directly from their offices." Looking at her faded-yet-serviceable jeans with the tear in one knee, a patch of blood on the other knee put there an hour earlier when Mori helped bring Morocco's new foal into the world, Mori knew she could never compete with the Queensly woman. Not that she wanted to.

As Mark and Shawna drove out of the yard, Cecile Riding, Mori's partner, drove in. Despite the fifteen years difference in their ages, Cecile and Mori complemented each other as business partners. The pint-sized Mori and the solid and hefty Cecile had a no-nonsense, yet compassionate, way with animals. When Cecile's husband died after draining most of their savings through no fault of his own—cancer—Cecile needed a partner. Lucky for both of them, Mori had some money from the sale of the house she owned with Frank and could obtain a loan to make it happen.

Mori waved before leading the filly to the south pasture. "Time enough to start working you tomorrow. Let you get acquainted with the farm," Mori said. The little chestnut filly threw back her head catching Mori by surprise and upsetting her balance. She stumbled after the mare, who backed into the barn door.

Gripping the halter rope under the filly's chin, Mori gained control of the animal. "You don't get away with that," Mori said. She put her hand out to rub the horse's neck to calm her before leading her to the pasture.

After releasing the young horse, Mori stopped at the barn to check Morocco and her new colt, then hurried to the office to see Cecile. When she was a young child she had ridden her bicycle to Riding Farm to see the colts. In time, Cecile and her husband, Ben, hired Mori to clean stalls, feed the Arabians, and eventually train and ride them in horse shows. Mori never lost her childhood love for horses, even during the years she attended the university to study interior design, and later in Omaha while she was married to Frank. It seemed fitting that she was back at Riding Farm, home in Colorado. Plus, she was grateful to be on her own and away from Frank. He hated everything to do with horses.

"Mark didn't waste time getting his horse out here. I'm sorry he caught you by surprise, but I was so busy I couldn't call sooner," Cecile said when Mori walked into the office. Her blue eyes, high cheekbones, and slightly arched nose were framed by an unruly mass of gray hair.

Mori shrugged as she seated herself in a chair across the desk from Cecile.

"Well, tell me. Don't keep me in suspense. What did he say?" Cecile impatiently tapped her pencil in the palm of her hand. "I'm dying of curiosity."

"He'll bring us more business, I guess. If we do a good job with Sunny Day, he has three more horses that he'd like to board and have trained." Mori grinned.

"He did? He talked to me about boarding her and training her at the chamber luncheon but didn't mention other horses. I told him you'd be in charge." Cecile chuckled to herself and continued, "He spent the rest of our time together trying to talk me down in fees."

"Tight, huh?" Mori asked.

"Well, sort of. He said since he wasn't sure of your experience and capabilities, he thought we should give him a discount." Cecile's face filled with amusement.

Mori bristled. Her voice came out high and sharp. "His nerve. Who does he think he is just because he's got money? I hope you didn't."

"Of course not. I told him that you are an excellent trainer and so am I. And like you said, he has more money than he knows what to do with, so he can pay for the best and that's us." She looked at Mori with appreciation in her eyes.

"Well, it's our good luck he's asked us." Mori didn't see the smile that formed at the corner of Cecile's eyes or notice the bit of satisfaction in her expression. "Can't believe he came all gussied up. Not exactly clothes for working horses."

"You had a bad first impression. Actually, he's a decent sort." Cecile swung around in her chair and stood. "How about some coffee?"

Getting off the subject, Mori mentioned Morocco's new foal. "Wait till you see him. He is perfect. Already filled out, and he was on his feet within the hour."

An orange school bus stopped at the gate, interrupting their conversation. A small dark-haired girl jumped off and ran up the driveway. Mori bounded from the office to greet her daughter. Love and pride filled her heart as she watched Emily pause long enough to pet the black and white collie-shepherd dog who met her halfway up the drive.

Waving at her mother, Emily continued toward her, swinging her small bookbag on one arm and petting Punch with the other. When she reached the office, Mori picked up the seven-year-old and swung her around before landing her back on the ground.

"We have a surprise for you," Mori said, planting a kiss on Emily's forehead.

"Morocco had her baby. Wow! Hi, Cecile." Abandoning her usual hug for Cecile, she tossed her pack on the office steps and raced toward the barn.

"Hold it," Mori said. "You should change your clothes before you see the new colt."

"Mom, I haven't got time. This is important."

"You're right. Let's go to the barn." Watching Emily brought a bubble of happiness to Mori and she glowed with contentment.

Cecile laughed as Emily beelined toward the corral, followed by her dog.

"I'm lucky to have the two of you with me," Cecile said.

Mori put her arm around Cecile and gave her a hug.

"I was so lonesome after Ben died, I didn't think I wanted to stay here. When you offered to buy a partnership in my business, I was delighted. You two have made such a difference."

"You'll never know how lucky we are to be here," Mori commented.

When they reached the barn, Morocco stuck her head over the stall gate and greeted the trio with a slight whinny before gently lipping the sugar from Emily's outstretched hand. Emily peeked between the gate slats as Morocco nudged her colt away from the visitors. The newborn stallion was covered with black and chestnut fuzz. Mori crawled into the stall.

"Can I come, too, Mama?"

"In a minute. Morocco's nervous, and we don't want to upset her. She might decide to kick. I'm going to lead her into the corral. You stand aside with Cecile so we don't frighten the colt."

Taking hold of the mare's halter, Mori clipped on the lead rope. She murmured soothing words to the mare, calming her, and reached out her hand to touch the colt.

"Beautiful lady. You've got a nice baby. We're proud of you."

Morocco moved her head up and down, nearly catching Mori under the chin.

"Okay, girl. I know you're pleased, and so are we." She turned to Cecile. "If you'll open the gate, I'll lead Morocco out. Emily, stand back, honey. This colt is already feeling his oats."

Emily jumped up and down, ponytail bobbing.

"Stand still. You'll excite the animals," Mori said softly. Emily reluctantly did as she was told.

Once out of the stall, the young Arabian danced from one side of Morocco to the other, keeping himself hidden from Mori, Cecile, and Emily. Emily darted back and forth trying to see the colt.

"He's lively," Cecile said. Taking Emily by the hand, the two followed at a safe distance.

"His name's Traveler and he's going to be my horse, Mama."

Mori smiled. "What do you think, Cecile? Traveler sound like a good name?"

"Yes." Cecile nodded her head.

Glancing at Emily, who was holding her breath, Mori said, "He should make a nice horse for Emily."

"Absolutely," Cecile agreed.

The sun-beamed look Emily gave her mother radiated even more brilliantly than before, and Mori's heart somersaulted twice.

Because of the colt's natural curiosity, he eased closer to Mori, sniffing at her with a quivering nose. Mori was eventually able to stroke his neck. Emily watched her mother, then approached the colt quietly and reached out her small hand to let Traveler touch it with a soft lip. Under the chestnut black hair was the typical black skin of the Arabian breed.

At first Morocco pranced nervously from side to side, trying to keep herself between her colt and Mori, but Mori's soothing words soon had her relaxing.

Standing still, Emily whispered, "Nice boy. We're going to be friends for ever and ever."

The trio worked with the animals for some time. Then Mori led the mare and foal out of the corral and into the small pasture kept for mares and new foals.

It was late by the time the three left the corral and barn. Mori and Cecile checked out Sunny Day one last time before following Emily.

"I think she'll train well," Mori commented.

As they walked toward their homes, their hired man, Jake Johnson, came in from irrigating.

"See we've got a couple of strangers out in the pastures," he commented. "Morocco's got a nice-looking foal. Who owns the filly?"

"Mark Larson." Mori's voice came out more forcefully than she expected.

"Hmmm. Larson's. That's interesting. How come?"

"We're going to train her."

"Good for us." Mori watched Jake glanced at Cecile. "Can't do much better than that."

"No," Cecile responded.

"Before I leave, I'm going to turn on the sprinklers in the southwest pasture. Like to get the water on overnight."

"I'll check before I go to bed to make certain everything is okay," Cecile offered.

"Thanks. Then, I'll see you in the morning," Jake said.

Cecile stopped at the office. "I've got some entries to make into the computer before I go to the house for the night."

"Need some help? You've had a long day."

"No. You and Emily need to get home." Cecile gave Emily a hug.

With Emily's help, Mori fixed a quick supper of hamburgers and potato salad. After supper, Mori put Emily into bed, too late considering the next morning was another school day. Tucking covers around Emily, she felt pangs of guilt. They had spent too much time with the new foal, but the mother in her decided it had been worth it. She had so enjoyed watching Emily's delight with Traveler even though their routine was broken.

"I'm going to dream about Traveler," Emily said in a small voice as she drifted off to sleep.

Before retiring for the night, Mori straightened her house, put dishes into the dishwasher, and took a shower. Sleep eluded her. She thought about training Sunny Day and the first time she had met Mark Larson. She was riding in the Arabian Horse Show in Estes Park. Mark, who was also a competitor, had been surprised after his comments to her earlier, when she took second place behind him. He'd even come over and congratulated her.

The ringing of the telephone interrupted her thoughts. Mori jumped up and ran to answer it, wondering who would call so late. She grabbed the receiver. "Riding Farms."

"Mark Larson. Hope I'm not calling too late." The minute he said the words, he felt like an idiot. He just wanted to say more, but he had been flustered. Now he was flustered again and wanted to hang up.

"It's okay." She cleared her throat.

"I owe you an apology," he stuttered.

"Why?" Mori said, surprised at his words.

"Well, I was early. I'd told Cecile I wouldn't be at the farm until late afternoon so I know you weren't expecting me," Mark said. His voice was friendly.

"No problem. I'm glad to train Sunny Day." Mori said.

"Good. Well, I'd better hang up. Just wanted to make sure. I may try to get out tomorrow, see how things are going."

"Anytime," Mori said.

"Sorry to bother you. Good night." The line went dead.

In spite of her efforts to sleep, Mori continued to toss and turn. It was almost with relief that she saw the first light of day. Normally she liked to stay in bed until the last moment, but today she got up, put on her robe, and went to the kitchen to make coffee. With two hours left until Emily had to be readied for school, Mori took her coffee cup to the outside deck she had added to her home. Leaning against the house, she sipped her coffee and enjoyed the early morning solitude. She liked the longer days.

The mares grazed contentedly in the nearby pasture. Birds sang and chirped in the cottonwoods as the sun's early morning rays turned the lower slopes of the mountains to an orange glow. Trout churned the water in the pond as they hit the surface, feeding on an insect hatch. To the southwest, the sprinklers spread their spray over the hayfield, creating a multitude of small rainbows.

Mori sat in a lawn chair and rested her feet on the porch railing. *This is peace. This is contentment.* Achieving her goal to pay off her debt in the farm challenged her, yet added to her feelings of satisfaction. Watching Sunny Day cavorting with another filly, she thought of Mark and the energy she felt coming from him. The momentary attraction caused her to imagine having someone to love again as she once had loved Frank before everything went crazy, before their divorce. She sighed and sipped her coffee. *No, no more marriage.* Life was just the way she wanted it.

Chapter Two

As Mark drove toward Riding Farm, he thought about Mori Jordan. She had changed from the haughty sixteen-year-old he had met at the horse show. Mori didn't seem to remember him, but it had been fourteen years since he had seen her. He had been twenty-one at the time, spending his summer between graduation and law school participating in horse shows, traveling in his pickup, and pulling his horse trailer from place to place.

Mori and Mark were competing in the same horse show. Cocky and so sure she would win the national dressage test, medium level, had irritated him to no end. He had told her he did not think she had a chance to place in the show as young as she was. Even now he chuckled when he recalled her gasp as she attempted to find her voice to his comment. She had looked prim in her light-gray riding pants and black leather boots. She had worn a frilly white blouse with a blue jacket. Except for her hair that she now wore short, she still looked the same. *Strange I remember all of that.*

When Cecile told him at the chamber luncheon that Mori was her partner and was doing most of the horse training, Mark was surprised. He didn't realize she had moved back to Colorado. After visiting with Cecile, he decided to take Sunny Day to the farm.

When he met and shook Mori's hand, her warmth startled him. He gripped the wheel of his truck as though he could recapture her touch. Immediately, he pushed the reaction aside, afraid to unleash his feelings to anyone. The results left him vulnerable to hurt.

Shawna protected him from commitments. They were friends interested in their careers, not a permanent relationship. She fit into his present life as a companion. Some people were intimidated by her money and her work as a real estate developer. Although she could act possessive at times, it meant nothing. She had been a good friend of his deceased wife. They like parties, the country club, and tennis. Neither shared his interest in horses. Shawna hadn't changed but they were friends.

Mark turned his pickup off the highway onto the washboard road that headed west toward the foothills and Riding Farm. Anticipation took hold of him as he pulled into the drive that led to the buildings and corrals.

He wanted to see Mori. Ridiculous. What was he thinking? One hurt in a lifetime was enough.

No one seemed to be around. The farm was quiet except for the chirping birds and the far-off occasional whinny of a horse. He opened the truck door and was greeted by the loud bark of a black and white dog. At first Mark was undecided whether to remain in the vehicle or brave the angry protests of the dog. Then he noticed the wagging tail. Behind the dog, a little girl skipped along the sidewalk that came from a small house with a well-kept lawn.

"Punch, be quiet."

The dog ran to the child and placed himself next to her side, showing his teeth at Mark as he emitted a throaty growl.

Emily stared at Mark for several seconds before saying, "Hello. Who are you?"

"I'm Mark Larson. Mori Jordan is training my horse, Sunny Day. And your name?"

"She's my mom. My name's Emily. This is my dog, Punch. I'm training him to protect me." She placed a hand on her hip as she spoke. "He's suppose to go every place I go, but he doesn't always do that. He's just six months old, and I'm still training him. Do you want something?"

The dog stopped barking, wagged his tail, and rubbed against Mark's leg. He pet Punch before closing his truck door. Bending down to Emily's level, he rested on his heels in a squatting position, and said, "I came to check

on Sunny Day. I delivered her for training last week."
He held out his hand to Emily. She took it with her small
hand that was sticky from the chocolate ice-cream bar she
held.

"You're the one who didn't want to pay us our usual
fee."

Mark laughed deeply. "Now, who told you that?" He
asked with good humor.

"I heard my mom and Cecile talking about it."

"Well, I've never had them work with my horses," he
defended himself. "Where is your mom?"

"In the corral with Sunny Day. Cecile's in the office.
If you want to see Sunny Day, follow us. I'll take you to
her."

Emily skipped ahead of Mark, ponytail swinging
from side to side. Punch tagged at her heels. As they
walked under the limb of a cottonwood tree, a black cat
plopped down in front of Mark, startling him. The cat
gave him a contemptuous glance and one loud meow
before falling in line behind girl and dog.

"That's Witch," Emily called over her shoulder. "I
found her when she was just a kitten. She was so hungry, I fed her, and then my mom said I could keep her."

Near the barn and corrals Emily paused and spoke in
a hushed voice. "You have to be quiet from now on. My
mom's very busy and she doesn't like to be disturbed
when she's working a horse." Her brown eyes were
solemn. To Mark, they brought to mind Mori's brown

eyes. They held the same open expression with nothing to hide.

With fingers to her lips, Emily indicated that all of them—dog, cat, and Mark—should be quiet. On tiptoes, she headed around the corner of the barn toward the paddock, where Mark caught sight of Mori standing with a new colt next to her. She acknowledged them with a nod of her head. Mark's heart took a nosedive. He held his breath to bring it back in place.

Emily peeked through the rails of the corral to watch. "That's Traveler. He's my colt. His mom is Morocco, and she's watching from the barn," Emily whispered.

Mark rested his elbows on the top pole and listened. Mori talked continuously to the colt as she stroked the animal on the rump with her right hand. With her left hand she gripped a small, loosely fitting halter. By stroking forward at the rump, Mori discouraged the colt from pulling away from her. Mori ran her hand down one leg to pick up a foot that she held for a minute. She repeated this several times with the colt, alternating hooves. Mark admired her gentle handling of the colt.

After about ten minutes of continuous monologue, Mori released the colt and opened the door for Morocco. The colt and Morocco nuzzled one another. Morocco made a few deep chortles before reaching out her neck for a pat from Mori. She gave both animals a treat.

"Come in and see Traveler," she said to Emily. She acknowledged Mark with a nod of her head.

Emily crawled through the poles of the corral and walked toward Traveler with her hand held out. She stopped and waited until the colt came to her. When he did, she petted his nose. The colt backed away.

"Very good, Emily. Shall we let them out?" Mori asked.

Emily nodded her head.

"Okay, out you go. See you tomorrow. Take care," Mori said as she pushed mare and colt out of the paddock.

She closed the gate after the animals left and greeted Mark. His rugged frame and self-assured attitude took her breath away. In spite of a catch in her throat, she managed to say hello without her voice cracking.

"Mom, Mark's come to see Sunny Day. I thought you were working her."

"I finished with the filly." She leaned over to plant a kiss on the top of the child's head. "This is Mr. Larson, not Mark."

"He told me his name is Mark," Emily answered somewhat defensively. As quickly her voice changed. "Traveler really did good."

"Well," Mori corrected. "Yes, he did."

"I just love him," Emily said.

"Sorry you missed seeing Sunny Day's workout. She's an intelligent filly. I can bring her in from the pasture if you'd like, but I worked her hard and she's weary." Mori noticed Mark's silk suit, expensive boots, and striped shirt that were perfectly coordinated.

She thought his clothes probably cost more than she earned in a month.

Mark said, "Don't bother with Sunny Day. Sometimes I can get here earlier if you tell me when you work her. I'm in court much of the day right now, but today we finished early so came right out hoping I'd catch you."

He looked directly at Mori, their eyes meeting briefly. She felt a slight flush in her face as she said, "I can wait until you get here."

"I'd appreciate it, but only if doesn't put you behind schedule." Mark rubbed his fingers under his chin.

"We're going riding. Mom promised. Want to come along?" Emily interrupted.

"Emily, Mr. Larson obviously hasn't come prepared to ride."

"Like Dad? My dad hates horses," Emily explained to Mark.

"Well, I do like them. I'd like nothing better," Mark said quickly, not waiting for further protests from Mori. "And call me Mark."

Mori smiled slightly. "We're going to ride Western saddles on a couple of quarter horses that haven't been out for awhile."

"I'll get my clothes. Where can I change? Then I'll help get the horses saddled, if you don't mind if I ride one of the horses?"

"I have a horse that needs riding."

"Great. I'll take a minute and be right back," he said

in a deep voice. It sent shivers down her spine. What was wrong with her?

Mori swallow hard before saying, "You can change in the tackroom. It's empty, but I haven't gotten it cleaned out yet today." She thought that would change Mark's mind but it did not. She watched him jog toward his truck with pantherlike grace. A lump caught in her throat and took her breath away. He was a hunk, no doubt about it.

"Did you say something, Mom?"

"Nothing. Talking to myself. Let's get the horses saddled." Before getting the horses, Mori took off her worn work shoes and pulled on equally worn Western boots. She helped Emily saddle Gun Barrel, a small, gray-mottled horse that would do anything Emily wanted. Next, she led Midnight out of a stall and put on his bridle and saddle, struggling for a second with the bit that he did not want to accept. By then Mark appeared dressed in Toni Lama boots, creased blue jeans, and cotton chambray shirt.

"I'll help you," he said, coming to stand next to her.

She felt his nearness and noticed how tall he was. Awkwardly, she threw the horse-blanket over the horse, unsettled by his closeness.

"You can get the sorrel out of the second stall, and I'll finish the saddling. The mare's name is Ginger," Mori said. She moved quickly knowing she needed to put distance between Mark and herself. Mori watched him lead Ginger into the alleyway.

"Her saddle and bridle are hanging near her stall," Mori called.

Mark picked up the bridle and blanket and put them on the mare before lifting the saddle onto her back. Mori made note of how gentle he was with the horse. He talked softly to the mare while he worked.

Mori turned her attention to Emily and helped her with Gun Barrel.

When the horses were ready, Mori led the three away from the corrals. They mounted the horses and rode through the pasture to a trail that meandered toward the pine-covered foothills.

Creaking saddles were in contrast to the light wind that rustled young, green cottonwood leaves growing near a small stream. Mori rode Midnight, a surefooted gelding who was alert and agile and who stepped lively over the rough trail. Emily flounced after Mori on her pony. Mark rode the sedate, lowkeyed Ginger.

Now and again Mori reined in her animal to point out to Emily the new pasqueflowers, miniature white spring beauties, and deep-purple sugar bowls that were in bloom.

"I want Emily to learn to appreciate her environment," Mori explained to Mark in a soft voice.

Mark smiled and agreed with her. A silent camaraderie developed between the riders as they followed the trail that wound down and up shallow draws filled with the pungent smell of juniper, over hills covered with widely spaced ponderosa pine with a sweet vanilla odor, and past rock cliffs of exquisite hues.

Mori turned in her saddle to point out to Emily a doe standing in a draw with her young fawn.

Mori felt Mark watching her. She said, "Hope you think your horse is okay."

"She's an easy rider. That's a nice animal you're on," he said in a friendly voice.

"Midnight was a luxury. I went to a ranch auction and he was for sale. He's such a beautiful animal, I fell for him. When the bidding started, I got carried away and bid higher than I should. Then Ginger came into the ring. She's Midnight's sister and I couldn't see them separated so I bought her. I'm still paying for the two, but I don't regret buying them." Mori pet Midnight's neck.

Suddenly, Emily's horse bolted ahead of Mori and disappeared over a hill.

"Don't you think you'd better call her back? She's not in sight. You don't know who might be on the trail or she could fall and get hurt." His voice was distraught.

Mori stared at him in disbelief and then amusement. "She's a capable kid and in no danger."

"What if you're wrong? Children as young as Emily need to be watched." Mark spurred his mare ahead of Mori and disappeared over the hill.

Mori smiled and laughed to herself. He sounded so worried. Just like someone without kids.

She kicked her horse into a trot to catch up with Mark.

At the top of the hill she saw Mark and Emily some distance ahead of her. Midnight tugged at the bit trying to catch the other horses. When Mori reached them they were laughing, and it pleased her to hear the happiness in Emily's voice.

"It's getting late. We'd best turn back," Mori said.

Emily looked surprised. "We usually ride to the reservoir," she protested. "Why do we have to go home?"

"We started late. We have chores, and you have to get to bed. I'm sure Mr. Larson has to get back to town."

Mark interrupted. "It's another hour till dark. I'll help with chores."

"Another time." With effort she controlled a shiver that washed through her.

"Can we go tomorrow?" Emily asked. "This is fun."
Mori nodded to Emily.

"Will you come with us?" Emily asked Mark.

"I'm sure he's too busy," Mori said.

"What time do you get home from school? I'll try to make it. I've enjoyed the ride," Mark said.

They turned the horses around. As they rode toward the farm, no one spoke, enjoying the late-afternoon colors. The mountains were shades of purple that blended into a pale blue haze. Flecks of clouds turned vivid orange, ruby red, and turquoise. The hills darkened into a deep green. To Mori, it was a romantic time of day and she hated to see it come to end.

Upon arriving at the farm, Mark helped unsaddle the

horses and feed the horses. When they finished, it was dark. Emily was tired and hungry, so Mark offered to take them to supper.

"Well, that's okay with me," Emily answered. "That is, if we can go to McDonald's. How about it, Mom?"

A smile lit Mark's eyes at the request. He was about to propose something better when thoughts of his son came to him. Perhaps, had he lived, he would have chosen McDonald's. His eyes were tender as he looked at Emily. "Yes, McDonald's it will be." He turned toward Mori for confirmation. "Hope you don't mind."

Mori did not understand the sadness she saw in his eyes and the melancholy expression on his face. That sadness wrenched her heart, and she could not refuse his invitation.

"It's a special stop," she said.

McDonald's was busy when the three went forward to give their orders. Emily studied the menu with critical eyes before announcing the Happy Meal she wanted.

"You must think I'm some irresponsible mother allowing such junk food," Mori said. She lifted her chin defiantly, expecting him to criticize her choice just as Frank had done.

Mark laughed. "Hardly. Guess we're all entitled to junk food now and then." Once the order was completed, Mark said, "Find us a table. I'll pick up the order."

Emily led Mori to a table next to the window facing the outside play equipment. "Can I play till Mark comes?"

"Sure. Come when I call." Mori's words caught in her throat as she saw Frank enter McDonald's.

Emily jumped from her chair and ran toward him, calling, "Daddy! Daddy!"

"I'll be," Frank's voice boomed, "if it isn't my little family. What a coincidence. But knowing you, I guess it's not surprising you're here."

Mori cringed inwardly, but said nothing.

"It's my ex-husband, Frank," Mori said to Mark. She stood.

Picking Emily up, Frank said. "My charming wife and a new boyfriend." He put Emily down and made a mocking bow to the couple.

"Hello, Frank." Mori's voice was cool, almost hostile. "This is Mark Larson, one of our clients."

"Not *the* Mark Larson. Not the famous defense attorney." Frank tilted his head to one side adding clownlike attitude to his words.

"None other."

Mori gritted her teeth. Frank was the last person she wanted to see. Why did he turn up at such inopportune times? Mori cast Mark a cautionary look.

"Won't you join us?" Mark asked.

"Thanks. I'll get my order."

"Can I go with you, Daddy?"

"No. I'll be right back. Later I'll treat you to some ice cream. Save room."

As Frank walked to the counter, Mori had to admit Frank was a commanding figure. Over six feet, he was almost as tall as Mark. He had beautiful blond curly hair, average features except for his sharp nose that was too long. He dressed fastidiously and groomed his hair forward to take attention away from his nose that he hated. Arrogance and expensive clothes were worn in a similar manner, but she knew only too well how shallow he was. She wished he'd disappear out the door and never return.

"What are you doing here?" Mori asked Frank when he sat down at their table.

"On my way to a convention in Salt Lake."

"Frank lives in Omaha," Mori explained to Mark.

"Going to call you kids as soon as I ate. My luck running into the two of you. Love you." He reached over and patted Emily's back.

Mori glanced at Mark. Her mouth formed the word "Sorry."

"Daddy, come play with me. I've eaten all my food," Emily begged.

"Hey, you run out. I want to talk to your mom. Okay, kid?"

Mori saw the craftiness around Frank's eyes and wondered what he was up to. She prayed he wasn't going to raise the custody issue again. Emily stood, and Mori gave her a hug. "Have fun in the play yard. I'll be watching to see what you do."

"I'll take Mori and the kid home. Rich guy like you must have had enough of this slumming," Frank baited Mark.

Mark picked up his burger and bit into it. Much to Mori's relief, Mark did not take the bait. She knew Frank was the kind who liked to find and then zero in on another's weaknesses. When Mark did not react, Frank frowned, obviously perplexed. He was trying to humiliate and embarrass her.

"They're with me. I'm taking them home if that's their choice." His voice was cold.

"I'll get Emily, and we'll be on our way," Mori said, relieved to leave Frank.

"Thought I'd come spend the night," Frank said loudly. "Haven't found a motel. Give me a chance to see Emily since I won't be able to take her for two weeks this summer."

Mori gasped. "This is news to me. Emily will be so disappointed. When did you decide you didn't want her?"

"Come on. You know that I want her. Just got too much going on this summer. By spending the night I can see her." He smiled but the smile didn't reach his eyes. "Besides, I'll see her on and off. I've got some business in the area."

Mori groaned inwardly at the last bit of information. "No." She felt the eyes of the other people in the room observing the scene. Picking up her billfold, she stood and beckoned to Emily to come inside where Frank dramatically hugged her and told her he was sorry he couldn't spend the night.

The ride to the farm was silent. In spite of her words of disappointment, Emily fell asleep. Mori was sick with the anger that raged inside her. Mark would never take them out again. But, she admitted, she really didn't care even if she had enjoyed his company. Mori folded her arms tightly across her chest. She was humiliated and embarrassed by the scene with Frank.

Before reaching the farm buildings, Mori said, "If you don't mind, drop us off at Cecile's. We'll spend the night with her. She has a guest room, and we've stayed with her when I don't like to be alone."

Mark cast Mori an anxious look. "Are you all right? You're in no danger?"

"No. I just don't want to hassle with Frank should he decide to come here on his own."

"Still loves you?"

"Hardly. I'm sorry if you were uncomfortable with Frank. Frank is, unfortunately, an adolescent wearing an adult body. He wants to have his cake and eat it too." Mori sat still, her hands resting in her lap.

When Mark stopped his truck at Cecile's, Mori shook Emily to wake her so she could walk into the house.

"Don't wake her. Get the door. I'll bring her inside."

Mark carefully lifted Emily into his arms. Her head fell against his shoulder, bringing to mind the last time he carried his sleeping son to his room three years ago. Pangs of sadness mixed with feelings of guilt shot through his body. He yearned for a time that he could not have.

"Where does she sleep?" Mark whispered, as he stepped inside Cecile's house.

"Upstairs, first room to the left. Follow me. Watch your step; I don't want to disturb Cecile."

Mark helped Mori remove Emily's shoes and tuck her under the covers. Then he followed her down the stairs.

"Would you like some coffee?" she asked. Her voice sounded bland and devoid of expression. She did not want to reveal some of the confusing feelings she had. Her frustration with Frank, her reaction to Mark, her loneliness, were fusing into an upsurge of yearning to be held by Mark.

"Thanks, but I think you've had a busy day, and I have a court appearance early tomorrow." He paused and took her hand. "If you need help, please call me."

Her hand was cold and her heart knocked loudly. For the first time in years she yearned to feel her body against another. He stood motionlessly staring at her. He put his hand under her chin and titled her head slightly. His lips felt firm as he kissed her. It was a kiss unlike Frank's mechanical ones. Mark released her. They said nothing, but Mori saw surprise registered in his face.

Mark broke the silence. "Promise me, you'll call if you need anything." His eyes held concern.

"Thank you. I will," she said.

Chapter Three

The ringing telephone shattered the peace and quiet of the early morning. Reluctantly, Mori put aside the newspaper she had retrieved from her driveway earlier to answer the call before the noise woke up Emily and Cecile.

"Riding Farm," Mori said softly, wondering at the same time who would call at six forty-five in the morning.

"Mori, dear," her mother said.

"Hello, mother. I'm surprised to hear from you so early."

"Couldn't get you at your house so I took a chance you'd be at Cecile's." Her mother paused, waiting for a comment from Mori, but when there was none she continued. "You'll never guess who spent the night with us."

Mori swallowed hard to push the lump that rose in her throat. "Just couldn't be Frank?"

"How did you guess? But you know he's like a son to us," she continued in a defensive tone. "How can you be so cold to him when all he wants in the world is for the three of you to be together again?"

"Mother, Frank and I are finished. He only tells you that to con you. His affairs with other women aren't so much fun if he doesn't have me around." Mori inhaled deeply to control the resentment that was attempting to take over her mind. "And, Mother, you know how I feel about Frank staying with you."

"Well, Frank told me how you embarrassed him last night. He is so vulnerable, so humble, I just couldn't turn him away. He was hurt by your actions. He's changed."

"Mother, I have to get going. What is it you want of me?"

"Frank wants to see you and Emily. He'd like to stay over another day with you. Is that too much to ask?"

"Yes, it is. He can't stay." Mori sighed. She loved her mother but she wished she wasn't always trying to re-unite Frank with her.

"But Emily is his child too."

"I know and Emily loves him. He can pick her up after school." Mori hesitated. "Did he bother to inform you that he isn't taking her for his usual two weeks?"

"He's working so hard to get ahead. That's why he can't take Emily for his time this summer." Mori heard her mother's intake of breath. "He deserves another chance. Your father and I would be so happy to see you as a little family again."

"Mother, it isn't going to be," Mori said firmly.

"Here's Frank. He wants a word with you."

Before Mori could hang up she heard Frank's voice filled with just the proper degree of concern and seriousness that was so familiar to her.

"Honey, please give me a chance. You're not being fair. You know how I feel about you and Emily. Come on. Let me spend the day." He spoke with all the charm of a victim in a harsh world. It made Mori wince.

"Look, I've got work to do. If you want to come and take Emily from school for the day, it's up to you. We've got nothing to discuss." Mori turned and saw Emily leaning against the door, listening to the conversation.

"Here's your father," Mori handed the telephone to Emily.

"Hullo." Emily's voice sounded so forlorn. She watched Emily's expression as it turned from joy to sadness.

"Okay, Daddy. It's better if I don't miss school," her voice filled with disappointment. "He wants to talk to you again, Mama."

"Well," Mori's voice carried her annoyance.

"Guess, if you won't see me," Frank grumbled, "I'll be on my way but I'm not giving up. I want you back. I'll expect to see both you and Emily in a couple of weeks."

"Don't count on it."

Mori turned toward Emily, whose face was flushed with disappointment and confusion. "If you'd let Daddy come here I'd get to see him. You're mean, mean, mean." Emily stomped up the stairs to the bedroom, arms swinging back and forth violently. For the moment Mori knew it was best to leave Emily alone. She retrieved the morning news and stared at Mark Larson's photograph on the front page. He was standing with a client. She'd just started reading the article when her mother's telephone call interrupted her for a second time that morning. Pausing long enough for one last look, she read, "Defending attorney believes in innocence of monster killer." His eyes seemed to look directly into hers, and she smiled. She studied the photograph for several seconds before putting the paper down on the table.

Hurrying to the stairs to get Emily and take her home to dress for school, she took two steps at a time. Emily pouted all the way across the yard that separated Cecile's and Mori's houses. Once inside her house she sent Emily to her room with the words, "Hurry and get dressed and come for breakfast."

In her kitchen she pulled two plates and bowls out of the cupboard and banged them on the kitchen counter, grabbed spoons and knives out of the drawer and two glasses. Quickly she set the table, her thoughts on Frank and the anger she felt. He had a way with people with his skill in small talk and he could be self-effacing when needed, a master at telling people what they wanted to hear. With those tactics he tied her parents around his thumb so that they blamed her for the divorce. It was inconceivable to them that such an upstanding, sincere young man could have stepped out on her time after time.

Frank needed her, Mori admitted, but no more than he needed any woman to admire him and tend to his needs. Mori was no longer the one to do that. In fact, Mori was quite sure any future relationships she'd engage in were going to be on a social basis only, including one with Mark, should anything come of that. She would never tend to any man's needs, ever. After her encounter with Frank, she doubted she'd see much of Mark anyway. And, as her mother reminded her from time to time, "You're nearly thirty-one with a seven-year-old. Not many men around who want to take on that responsibility."

With the table set for breakfast, Mori went to Emily's room to see if she was dressed for school. She found her small daughter sitting on a stool playing with her Barbie doll. When Mori entered, Emily looked up with a hateful expression. Mori ignored it.

"You'll have to hurry. It's getting late," Mori took Emily's lavender dress from the closet.

"I'm not going to wear that."

"What do you want then?"

Emily stomped to her closet and took out a green jumper and white blouse and put them on. After Emily dressed and brushed her teeth, Mori combed her hair, pulling it into a ponytail.

"Let's eat."

"I'm not hungry."

"I don't want you to go to school with an empty stomach." Mori gave Emily a hug.

"Okay." Emily marched to the kitchen and banged the chair against the table as she pulled it out. Mori did not scold her.

They ate in silence. After eating, Mori handed Emily her lunch money and walked to the bus stop with her.

Although Mori needed to get to work after Emily left, she grabbed the newspaper and took time to read the article about Mark and his client, Ron Miller. The descriptions were horrific. Ron Miller showed no remorse. Mark believed the man shouldn't go to prison. How could Mark even defend such a man?

Disgusted, Mori put the paper onto her recycling stash and straightened her house. She admitted she was compulsive about keeping it clean just as she was with the stables. Thoughts of Mark and Frank collided in her mind. On the surface, they seemed so different. When the house was in order, she hurried to the office.

"Morning, Cecile. I hope you didn't mind our staying with you last night."

"My no. I didn't hear you come in, and I barely heard you leave. Sorry I missed having breakfast with the two of you."

"I hated to wake you."

"Frank in town?"

"Yes."

Cecile shook her head in resignation. "Well, to cheer you up, we have another horse coming today for boarding and training."

"Who's the new client?"

"No less than Shawna Queensly."

Mori turned toward Cecile, baffled and surprised.

"I didn't know she was a horsewoman," Mori said. She leaned against the wall and folded her arms across her chest.

"She told me she'd like some lessons to surprise Mark. She even purchased a quarter horse and wants you to train her," Cecile said. "Besides, she wants to surprise Mark and ride Sunny Day when she's ready to be ridden."

"Couldn't be she's after Mark Larson?" Mori commented casually.

"Could be. They're seen together constantly, but they simply aren't a match in my mind. She's wasting her time and his." Cecile picked up a pencil and then put it down. "Now Mark is a fine man. He needs someone more like you."

"Cecile," Mori laughed, "he's not my type. He even insulted me, criticizing the way I monitor my daughter."

"You probably took it the wrong way. He was concerned and with reason. A few years ago, he lost his wife and son in a terrible accident."

"Oh!" Mori said. "Actually, I thought it amusing, someone without children, but that's truly terrible."

Cecile and Mori spent the next hour doing paperwork.

They went over expenses and cash receipts, wrote three checks to pay for feed, the veterinarian, and the repairs done in the barn. Then they discussed a client who was behind with his payments.

"Think we should put a lien on his mare?" Mori asked.

"I'll give him a call today. If I can't get him to pay something, we'll take him to small claims court. We may end up owning a new filly."

Before leaving the office, Mori questioned Cecile. "When is Shawna bringing out her new horse?"

"She said this afternoon."

"I'll work Sunny Day after lunch until she shows up. Want to come see how she's doing?"

"I'd like to, but first I've got all this bookkeeping to do."

Once Mori began her exercises with the horses she forgot everything else. It wasn't work. It was pleasure and relaxation. Often she forgot to stop for lunch as she put the horses through their paces. Time simply flew. When she was interrupted, she was disappointed. She enjoyed the work so much more than sitting in an office working as a secretary, as she had done before coming to Riding Farm.

Mori utilized the horse's phenomenal memory to her advantage, making certain that the experiences she gave each horse were those the horse should remember. She used rewards or punishments immediately after any good or bad action by the horse. Her rewards were usually pats and encouraging words. Rarely did she inflict punishment, but when some minor disobedience occurred, she admonished the animal with a warning tone of voice. The placement of her hands and the amount of pressure she used, were usually sufficient reward or punishment. She believed that horses were not born mean, but became mean because of the way they were handled and Mori considered each animal's temperamental characteristics, likes and dislikes, in her training.

Since Shawna had not arrived, Mori spent fifteen minutes with Traveler, putting him through the exercises of the previous day. Next, she caught a young sorrel gelding she was teaching to lead after she saddled and bridled him. She ran the stirrup irons up the leather to prevent them from swinging out or catching in corners, frightening the horse.

During her first exercise with him, Mori led him with the reins held six inches from the bit. She walked forward without looking at the gelding. He performed well. Next Mori lifted the reins over the horse's head. Holding them in her right hand close to the bit, she continued to lead the horse around the corral without resistance from him. When Mori finished Jake came into the corral, and she turned the horse over to him to groom, feed, and take to the pasture while she put tack away and checked the mares in the paddock.

She waited until three in the afternoon before beginning her work with Sunny Day. Surprised Shawna had not arrived for her lesson, Mori worked with the filly teaching her to circle at a walk, trot, and canter and to start and stop on command on a longeing rein without the use of a restraining line. She worked Sunny as long as she could, hoping Mark would come to the farm. Once she thought she heard a truck on the road and her body tensed in anticipation of seeing him, but it was the school bus dropping Emily off. Disappointment flowed through her body.

Emily arrived at the corral, excited about a school spelling contest. She skipped saying "hello" asking instead, "Will you help me with my words and give me a whole bunch that I don't even know?"

"I will and I'll think up some really hard ones. Let's take Sunny to the pasture and check Traveler and then go to the house. You'd better talk to him if he's going to be your animal."

Finishing with the horses, they hurried to the house. Mori stuck a casserole in the oven and suggested Emily study her word list plus several she wrote down while she showered.

It relaxed Mori, especially when she was tired, to shower and shampoo her hair after working the animals for the day. She stayed under the warm water as long as she could. Once out of the shower she ran a comb through her short curly hair, pulled on a blue sweat suit, pushed her small feet into a favorite pair of sandals, and went into the dining room.

"Mama, I know every word. Will you give me the list and don't do them in order?"

"Okay." Mori's heart filled with joy as she looked at her petite daughter. In a gentle voice she read the words, checking them off as Emily spelled them.

"Good girl. You earned one hundred percent. Let's eat dinner. Want to sit on the porch or in here?"

"Inside. I'll set the table. Then will you give me more words while we eat?"

"I'll really have to think up some hard ones."

"Mama, if I do my best then I get to go to the district spelling contest. Will you come and see me?"

"I wouldn't miss it." Mori carried the steaming dish of cowboy goulash to the table, brought out a cold vegetable salad, poured milk for Emily, and a cup of tea for herself.

"We'd better say a blessing, Mama, if I'm going to win."

"You say one." Mori folded her hands and bowed her head.

"Bless Mama, Daddy, Grandma, Grandpa, and Cecile and please help me win in spelling. Amen."

Halfway through their dinner they were interrupted by the persistent ringing of the door chimes.

"Who can that be?" Mori's face registered surprise as she left the table.

"Don't know, but it sure isn't very nice to come right now at suppertime."

Mori opened the door with a scowl that quickly turned to astonishment when she saw the bell ringer.

"Hello," Mark said. He smiled, his gray eyes looking directly into her brown ones. "Sorry I couldn't get here earlier. Hope you don't mind but Shawna said she was going to surprise me and learn to ride. She needed my help with a quarter horse she purchased today, so told me. He's in the trailer. May we leave him tonight?" His words flowed quickly, his tone pleading.

"She told me, but I didn't expect the horse until the end of the week," Mori said. A mechanical smile appeared on her lips.

"I know it's an imposition," Mark continued to break the strained silence that developed between them, "but it took longer to get the horse loaded than I thought it would."

"Hi, Mark," Emily brushed past Mori. "Can you come in? I'm going to be in a spelling contest."

"That's good news." Mark bent down to Emily's level. "Can you spell, mmm, I know, *coalition*?"

"Emily, not now. Mark wants to deliver a horse and be on his way," Mori said.

"But I can spell it. C-O-A-L-I," Emily furrowed her brow sounding the word out loud before continuing, "T-I-O-N."

"Put her there, partner." Mark offered his hand to Emily.

"Emily, finish your supper and get ready for bed while

I help him with his horse. I'll be back in a short time to read to you." To Mark she added, "If you'll come in, I'll change my shoes and get a jacket."

"He can give me my spelling words." Emily said. She ran to the table to get the list.

Mark read over the list. "These are hard words. You think you can spell all of them?"

"Try me." Emily sat on the edge of a chair, back straight, hands folded in her lap.

Within minutes, Mori returned to the room with her jacket. "I'll be back as soon as possible," she said.

"You're quite a speller," Mark said. He followed Mori out the door.

"We usually don't accept horses after five."

"I apologize. I see you are busy," Mark said in a soft voice. He brushed her shoulder accidentally and Mori stepped aside, afraid of her reaction to his touch, and marched down the walk to the driveway where she came face to face with Shawna Queensly, who leaned against the vehicle. Her stance was casual and superior, her demeanor haughty and domineering. Mori suddenly felt deflated and inferior as she looked at the well-dressed blond beauty.

"Good evening," Mori said cordially. "If you and Mark will drive to the corral, we'll put your horse in the barn for the night, and I'll have you fill out a boarding agreement and give me your health certification." She turned and strode toward the barn with quick steps. Mark had to back the pickup and trailer down the road before he could drive to the barn. Cecile opened her door.

"Everything all right?" she called.

"Yeah. Mark Larson has just come with Queensly's horse."

"Rather late. I'll have to speak to him." Cecile chuckled and waved her hand.

Mori offered to help Mark unload an unruly roan gelding while Shawna waited next to the truck.

"As soon as we're finished here, I'll have you fill out some forms. We charge for board one month in advance," Mori said.

Shawna cast Mori a vain, arrogant look. "Of course. I couldn't make it today, but I'd like to begin lessons sometime tomorrow. Three in the afternoon is about my only time."

"You can call tomorrow when I can check my schedule. It's at the office," Mori answered.

Mori led the horse to the last stall in the barn. Mark followed. Then Mori stepped inside with the horse. The gelding, she judged to be about six-years old, had a white cross on his face, and three white legs. "Not good," she said to Mark. "Could have trouble with soft hooves." She rubbed her hand between the horse's ears. "What's his name?"

"Strawberry."

"Nice-looking animal even with those white legs."

"Shawna's never ridden. The horse seems to have a good disposition. Talked to the previous owner. Said that

Strawberry belonged to his daughter, but she's left home so he decided to sell."

Mori closed the door. "There's hay next to the barn. Would you please get a partial bale? I'll get water."

Mark glanced at Mori, smiled, and left to get the hay, leaving Mori with disconcerting thoughts that unsettled and momentarily left her off balance. Shaking her head to clear the uneasiness she felt, she went for a bucket. Returning with the water, she met Shawna. Her mouth curved into an artificial smile that irritated Mori. She thrust the water bucket at Shawna, spilling some on her cream-colored canvas jeans.

"Your horse needs a drink."

"What am I supposed to do?" Shawna's stare was indignant.

"Put the bucket in his stall. Here's your chance to become acquainted with him . . . kind of a first lesson."

Shawna stood holding the bucket, a helpless expression on her face before setting the bucket down.

"I'm hiring you to look after the horse. My lessons start tomorrow. I'm here to learn to ride, not to dirty my hands doing your kind of manual labor." She folded her arms across her chest and watched Mori's reaction with a smug curve to her lips.

It infuriated Mori but she took the bucket to the horse. "Poor boy," she said under her breath to Strawberry.

Mark hauled a bale of hay past Shawna to the door of the stall.

"About two flakes of hay will be sufficient tonight," Mori said.

Breaking open one string, Mark reached for a nearby pitchfork and broke off layers of hay that he tossed into the feed box.

"Mark, dear, you've worked so hard today. Do let that woman handle the hay and feeding and let's be on our way. We still have dinner at the club." Shawna's voice was demanding and demeaning at the same time. Mori cringed, ready to refuse to board the animal or teach Shawna. Then she thought of the income that would be generated and controlled her temper.

"By all means, Mr. Larson, do go along. I wouldn't want you to miss your dinner." She emphasized dinner.

Mark sighed. He shook his head helplessly before putting the pitchfork away. Slipping her arm through Mark's, Shawna led him toward the entry.

Turning to Mori, Mark said, "Sorry to leave you with this."

"Oh, don't be disgusting, dear. You know she's hired to do that work. You aren't."

"I don't mind. I enjoy it." Mark shrugged his shoulders and glanced at Mori apologetically.

Mori watched them drive away before quickly finishing with Strawberry. She talked to him and rubbed his rump with her hand to give him a chance to settle into his new environment.

Walking back to her house, Mori wondered why

Shawna bought a quarter horse from someone else instead of an Arabian from Riding Farm. She wasn't going to enjoy working with Shawna. In a flash, Mori understood her feelings as envy. She lacked patience with jealousy and scolded herself.

Mori found Emily fast asleep on the sofa, a book in her lap, Punch next to her on the floor. She kissed Emily's forehead as she carried her to her room. In the dining room she found that Emily had cleared the table. She put the remainder of her dinner in the microwave to warm it but wasn't hungry, so she disposed of it and put the dishes in the dishwasher.

After changing into her pajamas and robe, Mori went to the living room to watch the ten o'clock news. Just as she was about to turn on the TV, the phone rang. Mori jumped to grab the receiver before the ringing woke Emily.

"Hello."

"Hello. Hope I'm not disturbing you," Mark's voice came over the line.

For a moment Mori said nothing, and then answered, "Sort of. I was about to go to bed."

Mark chuckled. "I don't blame you for being annoyed with us but I'd like to take you to dinner tomorrow night as a peace offering to make up for interrupting you this evening."

"McDonald's? Emily will love it."

"No," Mark laughed. "I have another place in mind. It's a restaurant in an old hotel up the canyon, kind of out of the way, but with a fabulous view of the mountains. Maybe just the two of us."

Mori was silent for a moment, wanting to say yes, wondering if Cecile would watch Emily, still prideful enough to want to refuse.

"Well?" Mark urged.

"I'm afraid I won't be able to find a sitter."

"I've talked to Cecile, and she thinks dinner would be a great idea. She offered to watch Emily if you will go with me. Make up for the inconvenience I've caused you."

"I'd better check with Cecile myself."

"How about 6:30? I can't get out earlier because I have an appointment with a client. I'll call in the morning."

"All right."

Chapter Four

Dinner at the Blue Grouse Inn was more than Mori anticipated. The old hotel sat beneath a 14,000 foot peak, one of the highest in the northern Front Range. The carved east face was highlighted by the late rays of sun and the glacier at its base was a vivid orange. Because they had arrived early, the hostess, Leslie—who seemed to know Mark quite well—recommended they wait in one of the old-fashioned parlors where they could watch the sunset. Instead Mark suggested they walk along the trail next to a stream.

Stepping outside into the cold, Mori was glad she had brought her winter jacket even though it was mid-April. She hoped it would shield her and the wild beat of her heart every time she looked at Mark.

When they reached the footbridge over the stream,

they stood for some time watching the clear waters of the Fork River. The massive peak towered above them. Late arriving clouds swirled around the summit of the highest peak and the slopes of neighboring mountains. The contrast of the white snow and the orange-tinted sky was breathtaking. Neither Mark nor Mori spoke, not wanting to disrupt the quiet sounds of the water as it fell over rocks nor the murmuring of the breeze through the trees. Mori shivered and tucked her hands in her pockets.

Mark looked at Mori. Slipping out of his jacket he wrapped it around Mori's shoulders. His touch sent more chills through her body, but a different kind. For a moment he held her with his arm, neither of them moving.

Mori broke the quiet, afraid her emotions were running beyond the boundaries of her control. "We'd better go to the lodge. Our table may be ready."

"Leslie won't mind waiting for us." Mark did not release his hold.

"Without your jacket, I'm sure you must be cold and I already have mine." Mori slipped away from his arm and started down the trail. To Mori, Mark was very attractive, more than he had a right to be, in his blue canvas pants, red shirt, and dark blue jacket that she now wore. The wind ruffled his sandy-colored hair, adding to his masculinity.

To protect herself against her strange feelings, Mori held her breath.

"A penny for your thoughts."

Mori chuckled. "I'm hungry. I'm always quiet when I'm hungry. I'm surprised you can't hear my stomach grumbling."

"Not above the noise of this stream." He took her arm to help her along the rocky trail. Her heart thundered in her ears at his touch but she did not remove her arm from his grasp. Her feelings astounded her. After her turmoil with Frank, she was leery of putting herself in the position of being hurt by a man a second time.

They walked slowly, stepping over exposed tree-roots. Here and there a few lavender pasqueflowers and pink spring beauties covered the hillside. The smell of pine mingled pleasantly with the decaying needles and aspen leaves littering the damp earth.

Returning to the lodge, Mori and Mark entered the ornately carved oak doors to be greeted by the hostess and owner.

"Enjoy your walk?"

"Oh, yes. Beautiful evening," Mori answered with enthusiasm.

"Your table will be ready in a few minutes. We've been terribly busy this evening," she apologized to Mark. "Would you like to sit in the library? There's a fire in the fireplace. I can serve you something to drink. It should help to warm you."

Mark smiled. "Fine."

They followed Leslie past a staircase that led to a second floor and into a small room lined with books. A fire burned brightly in a stone fireplace at one end of the room.

"What would you like to drink?" the hostess asked.

"Hot tea would be fine."

"I'll have the same," Mark added.

Mori studied her surroundings. Red velvet drapes hung at the long narrow windows that framed the mountains to the west. A Persian carpet was centered over hardwood floors. Heavy Victorian furniture, tastefully placed in front of the fireplace, invited them to sit down and enjoy the fire. After the cool evening walk, the warmth of the room was more than welcome.

"I'm surprised there are so many people here. The lodge seems so isolated," Mori commented as she snuggled into a soft velvet overstuffed chair.

"Leslie and her husband, Max, are well known for their Colorado dinners. They've won several awards. Then, too, they have customers coming from miles away to take advantage of their bed-and-breakfast specials. The breakfasts are super. Wait till you try Max's waffles some morning. They are unforgettable."

Mori's heart nearly stopped at the thought of spending a night with Mark. She hoped Mark didn't notice the color that flooded her face.

To bury her thoughts, she asked, "How long have they been here? I don't remember ever hearing about this place."

"At least ten years."

Leslie arrived with their tea, saving Mori any further feelings of bewilderment about her erratic sensations in Mark's presence. The aroma of hot spices filled her nostrils as Leslie set the tea tray on a small round table.

"I took the liberty of serving you our hot spiced specialty," she commented. "Hope you enjoy. It's on us for being so tardy with your table." Before departing she checked the fire. Turning to Mark, she said, "We haven't seen you for some time." There was a definite question in her tone.

"Not because I haven't wanted to come but my schedule has interfered with pleasure lately."

"I read about your latest criminal case in the paper. Well, back to work for me. I'll have your table readied shortly."

"No hurry. We enjoyed the walk and this tea is delicious."

As she sipped her tea, Mori studied Mark's features without being obvious. She noticed the small lines that ran out from his eyes. Sadness sometimes crossed his brow, especially when he withdrew into himself as he seemed to be doing now. His silence made her feel that he was miles away from her and the inn. She wondered who or what could be absorbing his thoughts. Perhaps—she reasoned—he could be thinking of his deceased wife and son. Undoubtedly they had visited the inn in the past. But that had been a few years ago. With a pang of envy, she wondered how many times Mark had been at the inn with

Shawna and whether they spent the night. The thought disturbed her and she pushed it out of her mind.

Mark turned his head and caught her studying him. His smile transformed his features, his white even teeth contrasted with his suntanned handsomeness.

"You seem to have mentally departed the inn," Mori returned his smile but her voice wavered.

"I apologize. This time of day with the lengthening shadows and failing light makes me nostalgic."

Neither one moved to turn on a second light, both enjoying the fire. Leslie did so upon entering the room. "My heavens, you would think we were saving electricity," she chuckled. Soft colors radiated out from the stained-glass shade. "Your table is ready."

Mark tucked Mori's arm under his and followed Leslie into the dining room. Mori observed the other guests. She noticed Mark's gaze assessing her.

Their table was located next to a large window. The last rays of the sun turned the peaks dark blue and the cumulus clouds vivid shades of orange, yellow, silver, and gray, giving a tremendous depth to them. Mori was certain that no sky in the world could be as spectacular as those she saw from time to time in her state. The beauty caught her breath. She wondered how she survived so many years without the mountains.

Wearing the typical uniform of white shirt and dark pants, a young waiter appeared at their table to give them a menu.

"Would you care for something to drink before you order?"

Mori quickly ordered decaffeinated coffee. Mark seemed to smile—as though laughing at her apparent aversion to alcoholic beverages—and then ordered the same. His expression made her feel she needed to explain.

"I'm allergic to alcohol," she blurted.

Mark said nothing but she noticed a dark shadow cross his face. Then he smiled.

"You don't need an excuse with me." He picked up his menu. "This lodge is well known for its Western foods."

"I notice they offer buffalo steak and rainbow trout. I think I'll try the trout."

"An excellent choice. The trout are locally raised and can't be beaten for taste." To the young waiter, he gave an order for two trout dinners.

"I love watching the sun set," Mori commented as she took a bite from a large salad with delicious raspberry vinaigrette dressing. When the broccoli cheese soup arrived, she tasted it with pleasure. "Everything is so good."

The quiet hum of the dining room added to its elegant, pleasant, warm glow, leaving Mori with a feeling of contentment. "How is your case coming?" Mori asked.

"Well enough. We've been granted a continuance to look into some recent developments." Mori studied his face as he spoke. She noticed the faint upturn of his lip, which caused her stomach muscles to contract.

"I've often wondered how anyone could defend such an animal as your client seems to be."

He scowled and then answered her in a cutting tone, "Everyone has the right to a fair trial and in this country everyone is innocent until proven guilty. Surely you remember that from civic classes?"

The cold tone to his voice left Mori with the feeling that Mark could be relentless in upholding his ideals.

He continued, "I have very strong feelings about this and I'm good at my job. You're not the first to have wondered." He laid his fork down and looking directly into Mori's eyes, he continued, "I can't judge people charged with a crime. My attitude is that I'm not just defending that person, but I'm also defending our entire system. The state has an obligation to prove that what has been charged did happen. That is not always clear-cut." He paused, obviously waiting for an opinion from Mori.

Surprised at her reaction, Mori nodded her head in agreement. For as long as she could remember she had little or no sympathy for persons accused of serious crimes, assuming immediately they were guilty.

"Please continue." Observing him as he spoke, she was aware of the magnetism in his bearing and could feel his strength. His demeanor as he rested his hands firmly on the arms of his chair was slightly arrogant, as though he defied anyone, including Mori, to disagree with him.

"Well, I had a case not long ago where a nineteen-year-old man stabbed a fellow skater at the roller rink and the man bled to death."

"Yes, I remember reading about that in the paper," Mori said.

"The state charged him with first degree murder which would have meant the death penalty. Now a stabbing can occur thousands of times each year and the victim won't necessarily bleed to death and the charge won't be murder. It will be assault with a deadly weapon. Unfortunately, in my client's case, the victim died." His voice was deep and vibrant.

"Yes, I can see that. What happened? I remember there was a conviction but not what sentence he was given." Before answering he scrutinized her face, as though daring her to challenge him.

"The man pleaded self-defense. The jury couldn't reach a conclusion. They finally charged him with second degree murder that carried fifteen years. The defense lawyer, myself in this case, mitigated the crime. The crime, as the jury decided, was not so serious it deserved the death penalty."

"And you had no reservations about the verdict? A man did die as a result of the stabbing."

"None. I did my job. I mitigated the sentence. It was a fluke that the man bled to death because the medics didn't arrive quickly enough."

"But what of your present case? From the papers the man is obviously guilty." Mori became so interested in Mark's comments that she, too, had stopped eating and was startled by the waiter when he asked if they wanted him to remove their soup bowls.

Mark chuckled. "We've let it get cold."

"I'll get you some more." He took the dishes and soon returned with fresh steaming refills and drinks and then withdrew, but neither resumed eating.

"Obviously guilty?" Mark questioned. "If the jury had been able to reach a verdict that would have been that, but they couldn't because the evidence wasn't presented by the prosecution in a convincing manner. We were granted a continuance."

Listening to his deep resonant voice was like music to Mori, and she could easily imagine his effect on a jury. He demanded attention. She conjectured that he was able to become the consummate actor if the situation demanded.

"If you are interested, I have some further opinions about defense lawyers." His eyes narrowed, his brows drew together thoughtfully.

"Please continue. You are giving me a whole new perspective."

"When there aren't strong defense lawyers to protect the accused against strong prosecutors, and that is true in this community, police abuse can occur. They overstep their bounds and become adversaries of the people, the first step toward a police state."

Mori frowned about to disagree, but before she could Mark continued, as though to convince her of his stand.

"For example, improper searches, seizures of property, arrests and beatings can and do occur. Police become oppressive as do judges, which leaves no recourse to the individual but appeal, and that is extremely expensive and sometimes not available."

Resting his elbows on the table with his chin cradled in his cupped hands, Mark paused, looking directly at Mori as though expecting her to agree with him. Mori said nothing but waited for him to continue, relishing his attention and his nearness. His voice reminded her of the grave, dark tones of the viola. And like the tones of the violin family, his richness of voice sent tremors through her. She hoped for an answer that would satisfy her curiosity about his present case.

As though reading her thoughts, he said, "In my present case, the jury could not reach a verdict because the state prosecutors did not present enough evidence to convince them that my client is guilty as charged. They, the prosecutors, now have time to look for further evidence as to his guilt, but we also have the opportunity to prove his innocence or mitigate his crime. I've found jurors take their responsibility seriously. They want and demand irrefutable evidence. It is a good system."

"So what happens now?"

"We go back to court in two weeks."

"And what are your chances?"

"I can't outguess a jury."

Their dinner came, putting an end to the conversation. Mori bit into the tasty flakes of trout topped with crab meat. She enjoyed the multigrained rolls and the snow peas covered with oranges in Dijon sherry dressing. The meal was concluded with baked cinnamon peaches and cream.

Finishing with dinner about ten, they went to the parlor to listen to the music of a local string quartet. Mori relaxed in the velvet-covered love seat. She sipped a glass of sparkling cider and enjoyed the violin concertos of Handel and Bach. When her shoulder rubbed against Mark's, blood gushed through her total being. She glanced toward him to see if he felt her reaction. His eyes met hers, then took in her face. She trembled with desire but quickly pulled her emotions into control as common sense brought her back to reality. She surely would not fall in love again and with a man who was seriously dating another woman.

They listened to the music until midnight. "I have a busy day and I really should be getting home," Mori said.

Mark seemed to take his time helping with her coat. His touch was soft and gentle. She felt a sensual warmth flood through her. Mark guided her toward his car. After unlocking the door, he stood watching her buckle her seatbelt. Her heart seemed to skip a beat. She noticed his shoulders heave as though he didn't want to shut the door. Shivers raced through her. Mark looked away from her, but she caught a spark of deep emotion in his expression.

It seemed an eternity before Mark settled himself behind the wheel and turned the ignition.

Mori observed the full moon that cast silver light on

Mary Hagen

the steep granite cliffs on both sides of the river. She studied the clefts and ledges of the rock, the reflections of the moon on the swiftly flowing waters of the river, the long shadows cast by the few evergreens that clung to the steep-sided canyon walls as Mark guided the vehicle around the sharp bends in the highway.

As they approached the roadway leading to her small house, Mori found herself in a dilemma. It had been years since she'd been on a date, and she didn't quite know how to act. Should she simply say, "Thank you for a fun evening," or invite him in for coffee, or what? Inviting Mark in might suggest the wrong thing, she supposed. If Cecile's house hadn't been dark, she could have stopped there and spent the night with Cecile and Emily. But it was dark.

Mark turned the motor off and laid his arm across the back of her seat.

"I had a wonderful time," Mori nearly stammered but kept her voice under control for once, not giving away her uneasy feelings.

"I had a great time too." He paused as though waiting for further comment from her. The silence was dreadful to Mori. She extended her hand to open the door.

"Let me." Mark reached across so that both his arms encircled her. Only the armrest and brake prevented him from doing more. With the door opened, Mori slipped under his arm quickly. Just as quickly Mark was out of his door and next to her. He took her arm to lead her along the walk. His closeness, his touch, sent her head spinning, and she felt lightheaded. The desire to reach out and touch him almost overwhelmed her.

"Where's your key?"

Mori dug around her purse, pulled out her key, and unlocked the door.

Before letting her go inside, Mark caught her against the side of the house with both hands resting above her head so she couldn't leave. Not that she wanted to.

Mark lowered his head. His mouth touched hers. It was a brush of a kiss, almost like that of one friend to another, but there was more. Mori felt both a longing and desire. Her mind went into a spin. It took all her willpower to gently push him away rather than putting her arms around him. She wanted to feel his body against her, but a warning in her mind told her to resist, for she had also sensed a coolness, a distance, in him.

Her voice cracked. "Morning will be here much too soon and I won't want to get up." Moving in a kind of misty haze, Mori backed inside her door. Mark watched her for a moment, critically studying her expression.

"Thanks again."

"Lock your door."

"I will."

"See you." Nothing more. She watched him walk toward his car. What had she hoped? she asked herself. His powerful body was illuminated by the silver moonlight. The passion she felt for him at that moment nearly overwhelmed her better judgement and she caught herself before calling to him to come back, to extend the night.

Chapter Five

It seemed to Mori that everything that could go wrong went wrong. To begin the day, Jake was at her door early to report that one of the yearlings was in a frenzy with colic. Somehow during the night the mares in the pasture had managed to pull some hay bales from the stack in the fenced yard. The colt overate.

Usually Cecile took care of such things, but she was on her way to Nebraska with three horses they recently sold to a family.

"I'll call the veterinarian," Mori told Jake. "Then I'll be right over to see what we can do."

"Not much, I'm afraid." Jake turned and headed for the barn, his body movements displaying his feelings of gloom.

Before calling the veterinarian, Mori woke Emily.

"You'll have to hurry. Eat some cereal and get yourself to the bus. We have a sick yearling."

Emily's eyes showed concern. "I can stay home from school and help you, Mama. What's wrong?"

"Thank you, love. The colt has colic, but you can help most by getting to school."

Mori was disappointed to reach Dr. Steve Dodge instead of Dr. Bill Corby, but she refrained from asking for Bill, not wanting to hurt Steve's feelings. Mori and Steve graduated from the same high school, had been part of the same school clique and, since coming home, had dated each other a few times. But Mori had more confidence in Bill's experience with horses.

"We have a yearling with colic," Mori reported.

"How serious?"

"I haven't been to the barn yet, but Jake claims it's a bad case. Can you or Bill come out right away?"

"Bill's not in but I'll be out shortly. I'm sure you know what to do 'til I get there."

After hanging up the phone, Mori checked Emily and gave her a hug and a kiss. "I really appreciate your getting ready for school alone," Mori said.

"Mom, I don't mind. It's not like I'm a little kid anymore. I'm seven."

Mori hid the smile she felt. "Have a good day at school." Mori rushed outside. The day was unusually muggy and the sky was overcast. *Well, she thought, we can always use rain.*

Jake had the yearling in a roomy boxstall. The young

animal's belly was enlarged. When Mori thumped the animal in the area in front of the haunches on the right side, she heard a drumlike sound that indicated acute indigestion. The horse was having difficulty breathing and was sweating and trembling in the front limbs.

Fortunately, Steve arrived within thirty minutes of her call. One look at the animal and he suggested they get her to the university veterinary hospital immediately.

"Doubt we can save her, but it's your best hope."

Without another word, Jake went for the pickup. Steve stayed with the yearling. With a feeling of depression, Mori followed Jake to help him hitch the trailer. Together the three loaded the young animal.

"Stay with her, Jake, and call me when you know anything."

"Will do." He pulled out of the corral with his hat placed firmly on his head, his shoulders hunched forward.

Steve put in a call to the hospital, but instead of leaving he hung around the barn, obviously waiting for Mori to invite him to the office for coffee. He seemed to expect it so, in spite of the many things she had to do, she said, "Come on up for some coffee, and I'll write you a check."

As they walked out of the barn, Steve noticed Sunny Day.

"What's Mark's horse doing here? You boarding her?"

"Yes."

"How come? He's got plenty of land up north."

"Said he wanted to train the mare himself when he has time and he doesn't have to drive so far after work, so he's keeping her here. I work with her mostly, however."

"Convenient." His tone was sarcastic. "See you've bought Price Sage's horse. Nice animal but I thought he wanted a pretty price."

"I didn't buy him. Belongs to Shawna Queensly. I'm the horsesitter."

At the office, Steve opened the door for Mori. His eyes assessed her with admiration. His attentions sometimes annoyed her and so did his nosiness about her business. He was too much like Frank. She reminded herself that he was an old friend so she said nothing.

"Hear by the grapevine that Mark and Shawna are about to get hitched."

Shocked by the announcement, Mori stood perfectly still, staring at the thermos but not seeing it.

"Something wrong?"

"No." She picked up the thermos. "This is yesterday's coffee. Hope it's okay." She handed Steve a cup and then poured one for herself.

"That Shawna's some good-looking dame."

"Yes, she is." His comments irked her but not as much as the pronouncement about Mark and Shawna. Collecting her wits, she sat at the desk to write him a check.

After settling himself in a chair across from Mori, Steve crossed his right leg over his left and took a sip of coffee. "Not bad for day-old java."

"How much?" Mori did not like gossip but it did sometimes serve a purpose, like this information about Shawna and Mark. Not that it made any difference to her.

"I'll send a bill."

"I'll be glad to pay you now."

"Naw. Forget it. This trip is on me." He added sugar to the black liquid as though he had all the time in the world. Mori glanced at her watch, noting it was not yet eight o'clock. Steve watched her but made no effort to leave.

"Look's like you're pretty busy."

"Business has improved." Mori leaned back in the chair, doing little to encourage conversation. Her answers to his comments were short, but he refused to take the hint that she wanted him to leave.

Steve was good-looking in his way, medium build, brown straight hair, hazel eyes with long black lashes. In the past, before she married Frank, they had some good times together. She knew from his attentions he had more than a passing interest in her, especially since his recent divorce.

Why, she wondered as she listened to him, *did one person like another but that other person invariably seemed to like someone else?*

"Well, better be on my way. We usually start getting calls and clients about half an hour from now." Steve set his cup next to the coffeemaker. "How about dinner one of these nights?"

"Give me a call," Mori answered.

"You're too tense, Mori. You need to loosen up, go out

more. There's a fund-raising dance coming up soon sponsored by PETS to raise money for the Humane Society. How about going with me? I'll check the date and call you. It's a good cause."

"If I can find a sitter and get away, I'll consider it."

"I'm going by the hospital. I'll stop to see how the yearling is doing and give you a call."

"Thanks, but Jake is there, and if I can find time I plan to run in myself. Say hello to Bill for me. I was surprised he was out so early."

"He's on a fishing trip. Taking a vacation for a change. Be back next week." He picked up his black western hat. "We could take the whole weekend of the dance. I know a great place to spend the night."

Mori took offense at the suggestive tone in his voice. Choosing to ignore the remark, she made no comment. Instead she ushered him to the door. He placed his hat on his head, ran his hands over the brim, bent down and planted a kiss on Mori's cheek, then slammed out the door. Once in his truck, he spun gravel as he wheeled his one-ton white truck out of the drive, unconcerned about the rocks he spewed onto the grass. Mori wiped the back of her hand across her cheek to remove the trace of his kiss.

No sooner had Steve left than Jake called. "Doesn't look hopeful," he reported breathlessly. "Just got her unloaded. Don't know if they can save her. Not much I can do here, so guess I'll come home and fix that dern fence so this doesn't happen again."

"Wait a little longer. Sometimes horses recover fast."

"Okay."

"Call me in an hour or so." Strapping her cell phone to her waist, Mori left the office to check the leftover hay pulled from the stack by the horses. She also wanted to be certain there would be no more cases of colic. The horses were scattered, contentedly grazing on the new green grass after eating most of the hay. The top wire of the fence dangled toward the ground. She picked it up and made a temporary twist around the second wire until she had time to repair it.

The sky continued to darken but no rain fell. Inwardly she wished it would pour so she could cancel her lesson with Shawna.

Mori spent an hour before lunch with Strawberry. His reactions to her voice commands, his behavior in his stall, his vices, and his level of training were important to know before she could let Shawna ride him. The disposition and training of the horse was excellent—too good for Shawna in Mori's mind—but she also realized Shawna could learn to handle the animal well enough. Obvious to Mori from the first lesson, Shawna had no compassion for the horse. She did not have the mental attitude to become an outstanding rider even with her athletic ability.

At times, Mori had difficulty maintaining her self-control, so important for a riding instructor to have. Shawna constantly tested her patience and her temper. During each lesson Mori tried to instill in her students a love and consideration for the horses they rode. She hadn't accomplished it with Shawna. There was almost a cruelty in Shawna's manner and in her treatment of the animal.

Believing that the impression Mori made with any horse was important, she put Strawberry in his stall, rubbed him down, and gave him some oats early, leaving herself time to change clothes. Mori put on breeches, a long-sleeved white-and-black pinstriped shirt, black leather boots, black cap, and dark gloves. Because of the muggy heat, Mori wore her shirt open at the neck. Her clothes were not expensive but they fit her well, giving her a professional appearance. Grabbing some cheese and crackers, Mori was ready for Shawna's arrival.

Shawna was stunning in the expensive outfits she wore for lessons. Today she had on canary-colored breeches, a pastel shirt worn with a white stock tie and diamond-studded gold tie pin, and a brown velveteen hunter's cap that covered the golden hair Shawna had pulled into a bun. The colors set off her blue eyes, which were made up with eye shadow. Her boots and gloves were of dark black leather.

Mori felt a pang of jealousy but quickly suppressed it. Shawna said contemptuously, "Where's Strawberry today? I expect to ride him, not this same nag you have saddled for me again."

"Strawberry still has a few habits I want to change before you take lessons on him. Although you're doing very well, he's a high-spirited horse."

Shawna frowned before asking disdainfully, "What is it this time?"

Mori cringed but replied, "He balks a bit and is slightly grouchy to cinch. As soon as he overcomes these things, he'll be ready to ride." She liked Strawberry and already felt sorry that Shawna was his owner. Galahad, a gentle gelding with an even disposition, never protested the mistreatment inflicted on him by Shawna.

With a disgusted sigh, Shawna grabbed the reins from Mori, jerking the head of the horse downward, obviously hurting the horse's mouth. Just as quickly, with disciplined firmness, Mori retrieved the reins, rubbed her hand gently over his nose, and talked to him in soothing tones.

"You seem to have forgotten that the first lesson at this stable is kindness to the animal," Mori looked directly at Shawna. "Remember he depends on you for his well-being and the development of his disposition. Galahad is a fine horse. I don't care to have him hurt by your handling. Anytime you mistreat him you won't get what you want from him."

"If that's enough of your lecture, I'll mount," Shawna said sarcastically. "And remember who you are. I will not have you speaking to me that way. I know well enough you're working for me. I'm the one in charge, and horses and people must understand that."

"You want your horse to be your friend not your enemy," Mori snapped. She handed the reins to Shawna and watched her mount with ease and grace, but once on the horse she sat stiffly.

"Since your ultimate goal is competition, you must relax," Mori directed.

Shawna cast Mori an impatient glance. "I'm quite relaxed. Let's get on with this. I'm in a hurry today."

Mori watched Shawna ride around the training track, making comments and pointers on how to hold the reins, her ankles, her knees, legs, and thighs so that the calf of her leg held against the horse. Shawna never seemed completely at ease even though she mastered the physical aspects of the lesson. Mori fed her ego as often as she could. At the end of the lesson, Mori walked beside rider and horse to the corral.

"Keep in mind you need to feel what your horse is going to do," Mori explained. "Tomorrow I'll have Strawberry saddled for you."

Suddenly Shawna spurred the animal, riding him in a tight circle inside the corral. The horse nearly hit Mori with his shoulders, and she swirled to one side to avoid losing her balance. With a quick reach with her hand, she attempted to grab the cheek piece of the bridle, afraid the horse might suffer a stress injury, so tightly was Shawna turning the horse. Just as quickly Shawna pulled the horse to a stop.

"How about that for a show," Shawna called.

"A bit hard on that horse," Mori heard Mark's voice.

Shawna thrust her lower lip out in a pout. "You're disappointing me. I hoped you'd compliment my riding."

Mori turned to stare at Mark, afraid he might undermine her lessons on kindness to the animal. Crawling through the corral poles, he came over to the horse. "I'd have thought Mori would have explained the importance of humane treatment."

"She harps on it. How could what I've just done hurt this dumb animal?"

"The horse was hyperextending his pivot foot. You also could have hurt Mori."

For once Shawna seemed subdued. "Mark, I just wanted to show off a little for you. You know I wouldn't want to hurt a flea." Shawna put her arms out and jumped from the horse, forcing Mark to catch her. They stood with their arms encircling one another. Watching from the sideline, Mori's mouth parted in surprise.

"It was sweet of you to come out today."

"Court was dismissed early."

"That dreadful case. It's beneath your talents."

"No. It's challenging."

Shawna reached up and caught Mark's face between her hands to plant a kiss firmly on his lips. "You are a soft touch, darling. I'm off. I have an appointment. I'll be home about eight. See you then." She kissed him again before leaving the corral.

The phone interrupted Mori's trance. She removed it from her belt as she led Galahad toward the barn, feeling self-conscious that she witnessed the behavior of the two lovers.

"Riding Farm," Mori answered.

Mark caught up with Mori in time to see her distressed expression and hear her say, "I'll come right away."

"Anything wrong?"

"That was a call from the school principal. Emily is sick, and I have to go get her."

"Let me handle the horse."

Mori paused at the entrance to the barn. "Thank you. He goes in the third stall. There are some oats for him in the feed can at the end of the alleyway. Oh, I usually brush him before letting him out in the pasture. You can leave his saddle in his stall. I'll put it away later."

"Be on your way."

"I hate doing this to you but Jake went back to town. We had a yearling with colic but she's coming out of it. He is hoping to bring her home later today. I'll be back shortly. I know you want to ride Sunny Day."

"Don't worry. I find this relaxing and enjoy it."

"Thanks again." Mori hurried to her pickup, half-angry she hadn't made Shawna take care of Galahad. She looked back at Mark as she drove past the corral. He was watching her. His expression seemed clouded with worry. Mori wondered what could cause such a sudden change in his mood. Maybe something went wrong at his trial. She waved as she drove out of the yard, not hearing his words, "Drive carefully."

Going as fast as she dared, Mori arrived at the school and ran inside to pick up Emily.

"I think she'll be okay. We've had a rash of one-day flu this week," the principal said as Mori put on Emily's coat.

On the way home, Emily dozed. When they arrived,

Mori helped Emily into her pajamas and tucked her into bed, hoping sleep would speed up her recovery. She took Emily's temperature and gave her a kiss. "I need to check the horses so I'll be out for a little while."

"I'm not so sick to my stomach anymore, Mama."

Casting a glance at the clock, Mori emitted a low groan. Almost four. With the beginning of a light rain and falling temperature, Mori grabbed her rain jacket and changed into her mud boots. Before she reached the door, there was a knock. She opened it to face Mark. His hair was matted from the rain and his shoulders were hunched against it.

"Stopped to see how Emily is feeling and to let you know Jake got back with the yearling. She's better. I helped him with the chores so you won't need to go out."

Mori hesitated for a moment. "Please come in. You're soaked." Feeling stimulated but jittery with Mark so close to her, Mori gulped to find her voice. "Emily may have a touch of stomach flu that is going through the school. She just went to bed, and you caught me leaving for the barn. I think I'm going to have to hire you to work for us." She laughed.

Mark tucked his hands into the pockets of his jeans. "Might not be a bad idea. I'll expect minimum wage," he grinned.

Her voice had been stiff but now it softened. "How about some make-do supper. That's our top pay at the moment."

"Sounds perfect."

She hung her jacket in the closet. "I'll get a towel for you to dry yourself. Come into the living room."

He followed her through a small, neat kitchen, the dining room with a round antique oak pedestal table, and into the living room. She stooped to light the gas grate in the fireplace.

"Stand here while I get the towel. The heat should help warm you."

While Mori went down the hall, Mark studied his surroundings. Fine maple paneling and a maple mantle decorated the fireplace. Above the fireplace hung an oil painting of a mare and colt, tails caught by the wind, ears pricked forward as though listening for some sound from the barn that lay off in the distance. Green grass was bent by the wind. Billowing white clouds touched with pink and orange raced across the sky. The painting was exceptional. Mark leaned forward to read the artist's name. A whistle escaped his lips as he read Mori's signature. He turned to warm his back. More paintings ringed the room. Scenes of wildlife and some of Emily decorated the walls. The room, though small, looked like something out of a house-decorating magazine. The blue-flowered chintz sofa and matching chair with antique oak end tables and stained glass lamps gave the room a homey country feel. His eyes roamed over the books that were in rows next to the fireplace, clearly displaying Mori's varied and wide-ranging interests.

Mori returned with a light blue towel. "Use this and please make yourself comfortable."

Mark ran the towel through his hair. Watching him, Mori felt her heart beat in her throat. She noticed his hands were strong and sure as he dried them with the towel. She liked that.

Catching her studying him, Mori turned away and went to the kitchen.

"Supper won't be much," she said. Aware he was watching her made Mori uncomfortable but excited. A warm sensation tingled through her body.

"Let me help." Mark threw the towel over his shoulder. "Tell me what you want done. Where can I leave this towel?"

"Put it on the washer. There are place mats in the buffet drawer on the right, silver in the middle drawer, and dishes in the cupboard to set the table."

"One for Emily?"

Mori shook her head. While Mark set the table, she mixed spinach, ricotta cheese, eggs, leftover chicken breast that she cut into small chunks, mushrooms, and spaghetti sauce. Next she made cornbread and poured it over the top.

"It takes about twenty minutes for this to bake," she said. "If you make the salad, I'll stir together an apple pudding recipe of my mother's."

"Sounds great." He walked to the refrigerator. "I presume the ingredients are in here. Do you have some olive oil? If so, I'll make us a dressing." Mark pulled out lettuce, tomatoes, celery, bean sprouts, and carrots. Mori set a bottle of olive oil on the counter.

Working with Mark thrilled and baffled her. She wondered if she wanted another relationship. Her feelings sent a wave of uncertainty through her just thinking about her life with a partner again. Turning abruptly, she collided with Mark. His body felt warm against her. She saw the color drain from his face.

Mori forced herself to draw away from him. She studied Mark for his reaction. His expression was one of bewilderment. She had a foolish, unthinkable longing for him, a feeling she wanted Mark to hold her, love her, desire her. She blushed.

Mark didn't move. He brushed her hair back and gazed into her brown eyes. She was surprised but not disturbed by his actions; she liked it.

The boiling teakettle broke their trance. Mori turned to retrieve the kettle. Mark scrubbed and noisily chopped celery and carrots. An awkward, uneasy silence rose like a sheet of falling snow between them.

To break the silence, Mark said, "I like your paintings."

"Thank you." There was a controlled tone in her voice, as though she feared she might betray her emotions.

"You are very good."

"Not really. I minored in art in college and I have an interior design degree, because I realized as I studied art that I was more clever than talented. When I have time I still like to paint as a hobby."

"I think you underestimate yourself."

Mori smiled at Mark and poured water over the tea bags she had put in her blue ceramic teapot. Frank had always thought her paintings were those of an amateur and not worthy of hanging on the wall of their house.

"Would you prefer coffee? It only takes a few minutes in my coffeemaker."

"Tea is fine. That casserole smells delicious." He carried the salad to the table, pulled two blue mugs from the cupboard, and set them next to the teapot. Mori watched fascinated, recalling Frank's complete helplessness with any kitchen or household task. In fact, he expected her to wait on him although they both usually spent the day at work. She appreciated Mark's help.

Before taking the casserole from the oven, Mori went to Emily's bedroom. She checked Emily, feeling her head with her hand. Her temperature was down, and she slept soundly.

At first, Mori was skittish sitting across the table from Mark. If he was aware of her feelings, he did not let her know. She envied his calm but then she doubted that he suffered from the same emotions she felt. When their hands touched as she passed him the salad bowl, her heart seemed to skip a beat.

Instead of taking the bowl from her, Mark kept his fingers wrapped around hers. They looked at one another, but Mori could not read his eyes or how he felt.

Mori looked down at her plate to collect her thoughts. She caught Mark's infectious grin, making Mori even more jittery.

"This casserole is delicious. I need your recipe," Mark said.

Mori looked up in surprise.

"Cooking is one of my pastimes. I'll have you for dinner for one of my gourmet specialties."

"Oh my. I'm certain this meal is no competition for someone into gourmet cooking!" Mori exclaimed.

Mark laughed. "Quite the contrary."

"I've never known a man who likes to cook."

"When I first married, it was self-defense. Denise couldn't boil water. I found I enjoyed it so I took some classes. It is relaxing for me, but I leave a messy kitchen." Mark's stare caught and held Mori's. He reached across the table to touch her cheek softly with his finger, sending a current of electricity racing through her body.

"You are quite beautiful, Mori, especially when color invades your face." He leaned across the table. The smell of his aftershave enveloped her, and she shivered with desire. Pulling her emotions together, Mori turned from him, jabbed a bite of food with her fork and put it in her mouth. She hoped Mark could not see her heart palpitations under her shirt. When she looked at him, she read uncertainty in his expression.

Mori stood up and went to the kitchen for tea. She removed the apple dessert from the oven. A battle raged within her between her common sense and her desire for Mark.

"I'll pour us some tea." Mark was at her side. He put his palm over her hand before taking the teapot. His voice sounded deeper than usual, husky.

Mori carried the pudding to the table, exhaling slowly, and sat opposite Mark. He leaned back in his chair and watched Mori closely. The pudding was untouched. They stood and moved together, and Mark's arms encircled Mori. She lifted her face to his. His mouth opened to meet hers. Then Mori pushed her body against Mark. She felt his racing heart, his strong arms about her, and she relished the moment.

"I don't know if I'm ready for this just yet." She pulled away from Mark.

Mark's look was one of puzzlement. She turned from him and quickly picked up dishes to carry them to the sink.

"This isn't like me," Mori said.

Mark gazed at her and took a deep breath. "Nor me. It's been a long time since I've let my feelings open up. But you're special. I like being with you."

"And I like having you with me," Mori said in a soft voice.

Emily padded into the kitchen barefooted and put her arms out to be hugged by Mori. "Mama, I'm feeling better. Hi, Mark. What 'cha doin' here?"

"Hello, dear." She led Emily into the dining room. Mori sat and Emily climbed onto her lap. Mark, watching the two, felt a heavy throbbing and churning inside himself, touched by the obvious love Mori had for Emily. It brought back painful memories.

"Hungry?" Mori asked.

"A little."

"Want some toast and tea?"

"Okay."

"I'll get it," Mark offered.

Emily smiled at him. "Are you visiting us or just checking Sunny Day?"

"Visiting. Sorry you're sick."

"Me too."

"The bread is in the refrigerator and the toaster is on the shelf under the oven," Mori directed.

After serving Emily, Mark sat down, unable to propel himself into leaving. He enjoyed the love, the warmth, and the coziness he felt in the home. The thought of returning to his house furnished in modern black and white, glass and steel that he'd never changed after Denise's death, repelled him. Yet, he knew he must leave, he was so afraid of his feelings.

Emily picked at her toast, eating only a few bites, still not feeling too well. She chatted with Mark about Traveler but then asked to go to bed.

"Okay, love," Mori said. "Let's see if I can still carry you." Emily put her arms around Mori.

"I think I'd better do the honors," Mark offered. Emily's smile as he picked her up melted him completely. "Which way?"

"My room is the first one down the hall."

Following behind them, Mori compared Mark to Frank and noticed how different they were. Together Mori and Mark tucked Emily into bed and returned to the dining room.

"I'll help clean up the kitchen before I go home," Mark offered.

"No need," Mori shook her head.

"I insist." He rinsed dishes under the faucet before putting them in the dishwasher. "How about dinner at my house tomorrow night? You and Emily."

"Can I let you know? It depends on Emily and whether Cecile gets home," she said as she walked to the door with Mark.

Before leaving Mark took her chin in his hand. Turning her face upward, he kissed her gently. "I had a nice evening. The best I've had in a long time. Thank you."

Outside the rain fell steadily. Mori reached for an umbrella resting in an antique cream can and gave it to him. He refused to take it. Hunching his shoulders against the rain, she watched him run to his truck. Her face burned just thinking about his touch and his kiss. She shut the door and leaned against it.

Chapter Six

Wind rattled Mori's window and rain spattered against it, waking her earlier than usual. She put on her robe and walked to the patio doors to look out. The morning was gray and dreary, the trees shadows in the mist. With a sigh, Mori turned to make coffee. The weather would cause cancellations in riding lessons that morning. Having lived most of her life in this semi-arid West, she appreciated the rain in spite of the inconvenience. Mori poured a cup of coffee, sat down, propped her feet up on a nearby chair to enjoy the softly falling rain for a few moments before getting Emily ready for school.

Looking at her calendar, she made a mental note of the lunch date she had with three friends she had not seen since her divorce and the time of Emily's spelling bee. The rain eliminated some of the usual rush to meet her daily deadlines.

A sleepy-eyed Emily shuffled into the dining room. She wanted to be held so Mori put down her coffee cup.

"It's raining. Can I wear my yellow slicker to school?" she asked.

"Yes. Don't forget it's spelling day."

"I won't. I'm so excited I could hardly sleep. Can I wear my denim dress and blue stockings and new shoes?"

"Of course. You'll look the best."

"Are Grandma and Grandpa coming? Is Daddy going to get here?"

"Your grandparents are, but I haven't heard from your father."

Emily slumped in Mori's arms. "You told him, didn't you?"

"Yes. Now we had best get you dressed."

During breakfast and on the way to the bus stop Mori asked Emily spelling words. Once Emily was on the bus, Mori hurried to help Jake feed the horses. Then she checked with Cecile, who had returned during the night from delivering three horses to a ranch in Nebraska.

"Glad you're back," Mori greeted Cecile. "How was the trip?"

"The trip went well and the family was pleased with the horses, *and*"—Cecile emphasized the word—"we have cash to put in our checking account. Have time for a bite of breakfast?"

Mori declined. "Had breakfast with Emily, but I'll have one cup of coffee. I'm going to meet some friends for lunch, so I can deposit the check if you'd like. Emily's spelling bee is this afternoon. Want to come?"

"Absolutely."

"I'll pick you up."

"No need. Enjoy your lunch. I'll meet you at the school. What time?"

"Starts at 1:30."

A chill permeated the air and Mori picked up a warmer jacket, cap, and gloves from the office before sloshing through sticky gumbo to the barn. Jake and she threw extra hay to the horses, made certain the colts were all right, and brought an expectant mare into the barn. Even with the rain curtailing much of the routine work, Mori was pressed for time to meet her friends for lunch.

They gathered at a tea house next to the city's largest mall. The waitress led Mori past a fireplace that added warmth and cheer to the room and to a table next to a large window.

"Our recluse has arrived," one of her friends greeted her. "It's been too long since we've seen you."

"It's not that I'm a recluse intentionally. I'm just busy, and it's hard to get to town. How are all of you? You look great."

The waiter pulled out a chair for Mori and handed her a menu. "I'll be back to take your orders."

Short comments were exchanged between Helen,

Susie, Nedra, and herself while they studied the menu. After the waiter took their order, Nedra leaned toward Mori, resting her elbows on the table. "We're waiting. We've heard you've been out with Mark Larson. How did you manage that? I've been trying for years to get him to look my way. I'm so envious."

"He took Emily and me for hamburgers at McDonald's."

"McDonald's! See, Nedra, I told you to beware," Helen teased.

"I'd think he could do better than that," Susie added.

"That's where Emily wanted to go."

"You're not telling us the whole story. I have word that he took you to the Blue Grouse Inn. Come on. You're holding out on us! I even joined the country club so Mark would notice me. I haven't managed to get past Shawna," Nedra said.

"Well, if anyone could get past her it would be you," Susie said.

Mori looked from one woman to another. They had been friends since grade school. Beautiful, sophisticated Nedra with her dark red hair, chocolate-brown eyes, and white skin without a single freckle had, at one time or another, swiped boyfriends from each one of them. Mentally, Mori counted the number of times Nedra had been engaged and then broken it off a week or less before a wedding. As a child, Nedra had watched her father abuse and beat her mother. Once Nedra told Mori, "I can't forgive my mother for staying with him." Mori never forgot the bitterness in Nedra's voice.

"Where are your thoughts?" Helen asked Mori. "How is your horse business?"

"Okay," Mori answered. "We just sold three horses."

"I heard Frank's been in town. I even saw him with Shawna," Helen continued.

The comment surprised Mori and she wondered what Frank was up to this time. She nodded her head at Helen.

"You still separated from Joe?" Helen asked Susie.

With an expression of astonishment, Mori faced Susie. "I didn't know. I'm sorry."

"Don't be. I've stayed with him too long. I just made up my mind I'd had enough."

"Susie has been in a shelter for battered women with her two youngsters," Nedra interjected. "She's just started working at Larson's Department Store."

"Oh, Susie, you mean Joe, the mouse we knew in school, has . . ." Mori exclaimed.

"The one. It's been terrible. I put up with it for the sake of the children, but when he knocked me out of my chair while I was holding Rusty, it was the final straw. I packed up and left and I'm not going back."

"Three cheers," Helen said.

"You've been through this," Susie said to Mori. "Divorce or separation seems, well, so final. Yet, I'm anxious to bring things to a close."

"Yes, I know the feeling. But I'm not sorry now that

Frank and I are divorced, even though at the time I thought I couldn't live without him. He wanted the divorce, not me. Now I know it was for the best."

Their lunches came. While they ate, the three women filled Mori in about friends, children, and jobs. She learned that Nedra had opened her own real estate firm, Helen was pregnant for the third time and not pleased about it, and Susie was looking for a house to buy, with Nedra's help. But it was Mark Larson who interested the group most.

"I'm so jealous," Nedra commented between bites of crab salad. "How did you meet him?"

"He's boarding a horse with us."

"Guess I'd better take up riding. How about lessons? What time is Mark at your place?"

Mori laughed. "Save your money, Nedra. Shawna's already coming out to learn to ride."

"Great. I know a name I could call her."

"Nedra, you are the last one I can imagine on a horse," Helen said. "Look at you. Hair, makeup, clothes right out of *Glamour.* You've never liked any athletic activities."

"As far as looks go, Nedra can definitely hold a candle to Shawna," Mori commented. "She's always dressed to kill. Maybe you should come to the farm and give her some competition."

"I'd like to be there," Susie said. Mori heard the fatigue in Susie's voice and saw how worn out she looked. Her heart went out to her friend.

"Why don't you bring the boys out soon. I'll saddle some horses, and we'll go riding."

"The kids would love that. I'll call when I can."

"Bring your two girls, Helen, and you come, Nedra, and we'll go on a picnic. And we'll make certain you face forward in the saddle."

"I'm pregnant, remember," Helen said, "and my two and three-year-old darlings would probably drive us all up the wall. Rick wouldn't be too keen on me riding during my pregnancy. Thanks anyway."

"Well, so much for that. I probably would get on a horse backwards," Nedra laughed. "Changing the subject, don't take Mark's interest in you too seriously, Mori. He may already be taken, although I doubt he'll ever take the final step. I did hear that Mark and Shawna have been house hunting and that Shawna's going to sell her condo and Mark is selling his house too. Wish they were my clients."

Mori's heart thudded loudly. She felt color drain from her face. She knew there was nothing between Mark and her, but still she felt shocked and disappointed. Her stomach churned uncomfortably.

"So that got a reaction from you. I can see by your expression. You do like Mark. Mori's not being honest with us," Nedra teased.

"Come off it, Nedra," Susie said. "Don't ruin our lunch."

Nedra pushed her plate aside and leaned across the

table, arms folded in front of her. In a conspiring tone of voice she said to Mori, "You'd better get your act together if you want to catch one of the most intriguing men in town. Need some help?"

"Oh, Nedra, you know as well as we, that Mark Larson likes conquests. No one wins with him," Helen said. "He's still recovering from the death of his family."

Mori laughed, taking a deep breath to control her feelings. "Maybe you should give him a try, Nedra. If you can take him from Shawna, go for it. I'll leave the field to you."

"Don't give up so easily. He's had lots of women on the hook but never married any of them," Nedra challenged. "And I'd love to see you beat out Shawna, not me."

"Well, I have to run," Mori said.

"What's your rush? We have so much more to discuss," Susie protested. "We haven't heard the full story about you and Frank."

"I heard he's around trying to patch things up between the two of you. That's from your mom," Helen said.

Anger surged through Mori's body. She controlled her desire to make a snappish reply. "Maybe he'll find Shawna more to his liking. You said he was with her." Mori slipped her arms into her jacket and picked up her handbag.

"Emily's competing in a spelling bee and I have to be at her school at 1:30," she said. "Nice to see all of you."

"We'll do it again. Oh, are you going to the Humane Society dance? Rick and I are, of course, because of his involvement through our business. Steve said he'd invited you. We could make it a foursome." Helen pushed away from the table.

"I haven't decided," Mori answered.

Nedra arched an eyebrow. "I'm going with John. Before any of you say anything, I know he's married but his wife is out of town."

Mori left without waiting to hear the anticipated protests aimed at Nedra. Stepping outside, she felt refreshed by the clean smell of rain. She unlocked the door of her pickup and climbed in. It took her thirty minutes to reach the school and find a place to park.

Mori was surprised to meet Mark on the school steps. Her heart did a nose dive into her stomach at the sight of him standing under the overhang out of the mist. He looked stupendous in his dark suit. He smiled.

"You look beautiful. The rain does something for you." He took her arm.

"Thank you." His compliment flustered her, and she felt color rush to her face. "I'm surprised to see you." Her voice sounded deep and unnatural to her ears and she caught the smile that played across his lips. "I didn't think you'd have time for Emily's spelling bee."

"I made a promise," Mark said.

"Emily will be pleased," Mori said. *Frank rarely kept a promise and Mark was here remembering he had told Emily he would come.*

"I just met your parents. Nice people. They're with Cecile and are saving us a seat."

The small gymnasium was full and smelled of sweat and gym shoes. Cecile spotted them and waved. Her parents turned with smiles for her, an expression of curiosity on her mother's face.

Once the visitors to the school were seated, the contestants marched in to take seats on the stage. When Emily located them she waved, then settled into her chair looking very small and vulnerable to Mori. She felt Mark's fingers entwine with hers. His gentle squeeze sent a tingling sensation down her spine. She didn't remove her hand but glanced at him. His attention was directed toward the students.

To rid herself of the tingles that plagued her, Mori removed her hand from his and concentrated on the young contestants as each word was pronounced and then spelled. Every time Emily spelled her word correctly, Mark turned an approving eye toward Mori, causing her insides to do another somersault. She pulled her focus around in time to hear Emily spell *disappoint*, her last word. Pride glowed on Mori's face as the audience applauded her daughter as first-place winner for the second grade.

After the awarding of prizes, Mori's parents asked to take Emily with them for the weekend.

"We're going to drive to Glenwood Springs, and we'd love to have Emily come with us," her mother said. "After all, champions need rewards. Don't you agree?"

"Can I go, Mom, please?"

"Sounds fun to me."

During the spelling bee the rain stopped and the sun was out. Cecile asked all of them to come to her home for hamburgers.

Mori appreciated Mark for attending the spelling bee, something Frank would never take time to do.

Emily smiled at Mark. "Please come, please," she pleaded with him.

Mark glanced from Emily to Mori for agreement.

"We'd love to have you join us," Mori said.

"Yes," Mori's father added. "Give us a chance to get acquainted."

"Cecile is a great cook," Mori said.

"Sounds like I'm in for a treat," Mark said.

"Oh boy." Emily grabbed Mark's hand and led him to his pickup.

"Can I ride with Mark?" Emily asked.

"I think that's up to Mark," Mori said.

"Absolutely." He helped Emily into his truck and buckled her seat belt.

At the cookout, Jenny, Mori's mother, tried several times to catch her daughter alone. Knowing exactly what her mother wanted, Mori avoided her as long as possible, but Jenny finally cornered her in the kitchen.

"Do be careful of Mark Larson. You mustn't take chances. Do take precautions. And remember, Frank still is a part of you."

"Mother, leave Frank out of this. He is not a part of

my life anymore and never will be. We're divorced, re-member?" Mori snatched a bowl of salad and stomped into Cecile's sun room. Why couldn't her mother under-stand? She and Frank were finished.

Emily fidgeted most of the meal, anxious to go home and pack her clothes. Finally, Mori excused Emily be-fore she had finished her meal to go and get ready for the trip.

"Come with me, Grandma. I don't know what to take."

"Well, some shorts, a bathing suit for the hot springs, some pants in case it's cold and a jacket too. Let's carry our dishes into the kitchen, and we'll go get you packed."

"I'll be over in a few minutes," Mori's father, Dave, said between bites of chocolate cake. "Good thing we packed before the spelling bee. We should be leaving if we're going to get to there tonight."

"Thanks so much, Cecile. You must come over to our house with Mori some evening," Jenny said.

"Hurry, Grandma." Emily tugged impatiently on her grandma's hand. She turned to Mark. "Thanks for com-ing to my spelling contest."

Mark squatted in front of Emily. "Thanks for asking me. You're a great speller."

Emily gave Mark a hug before following her grand-mother out of the house. As the child left the room, Mori caught Mark staring after them with an expression of sadness, as though his heart was broken. Mark pushed himself into a standing position to say good-bye to Dave.

After Mori's family left, she and Mark helped Cecile clear the table. More than once Mori's shoulders brushed Mark's, leaving her feeling bewildered. It seemed he was deliberately making body contact. Earlier that day, Mori had heard Shawna and he were looking at houses. What did he want from Mori anyway?

"Enough work, you two." Cecile took the dish towel from Mark. "Let's go sit." Cecile led them into her living room.

Mark lowered his six foot frame into a leather arm chair. "We're having a community rodeo and barbecue tomorrow at the ranch. Thought I'd enter the calf roping and bulldogging. How about coming with me, Mori?" Mark asked.

Gulping, Mori licked her lips, wanting to say yes. "Oh, I can't," she said. "With the end of the rain, we'll have riders out for the day and I've got to be here"

"Nonsense," Cecile spoke up. "You need a break. I'll look after the horses and riders." She turned to Mark. "Since Mori's become my partner, I hardly get a chance to work with the animals. It'll be good for me."

"I'll pick you up at six, if that's not too early."

Mori laughed. "I'll be ready. You forget I'm a farm lady. Six is late around here." Her heart raced and thumped loudly. She held her breath to quench the excitement she felt.

Looking at his watch, Mark exclaimed, "Too late for me to do any more work at the office. I have an idea. Why don't you two go with me to the Western Oyster Bar for some dancing? The Lone Star Band is playing. I know you and Ben used to go there quite often, Cecile."

"We had some great fun." Cecile looked from Mark to Mori. A smile touched the corners of her blue eyes. "I think it would be nice for the two of you to go."

"I can't go. If I'm going with you up to your ranch tomorrow, I have to stay here and catch up on some work," Mori answered quickly, caution mixed with excitement filling her mind.

"What? We've been rained in for the past two days. The office work is completed," Cecile spoke up instantly. Anything that needs doing, I can handle."

"I've been off all day," Mori stared at Cecile in an effort to send her the message that she didn't feel comfortable being with Mark alone.

"That's all right. You need some time. Emily is with your parents. Now hustle along."

Mark picked up her sweater and held it out for her to put on.

"Have a fun time. When Ben was alive, we loved going to hear the music and dance," Cecile said.

Before leaving, Mark thanked Cecile and gave her a good-bye kiss. Turning to Mori, he took her arm in his, grinning sheepishly. She trembled. Suspicion hit her. Had this been planned by Cecile and Mark?

The Western Oyster Bar was known for miles around for its delicious Rocky Mountain oysters and country bands. Dancers thumped to the music on the small floor.

Waitresses scurried among tightly packed tables with trays of beer and fried oyster chips. Mark and Mori followed a young waitress to a table that overlooked the dance floor.

"Want something to drink?" the waitress asked.

"I'll have a dark beer and don't forget the oysters."

"A Coke for me," Mori shouted over the din of music and laughter.

Because of the noise, conversation was difficult. Mark yelled, "Want to try and find some space for the remainder of this dance?"

Mori nodded her head, and Mark led her to the crowded floor. Taking Mori into his arms, he stared into her dark eyes. His touch made her quiver. To the beat of the band, Mark led her around the floor, drawing her close to him to avoid collisions with other couples. His warm breath on her forehead sent ripples of excitement though her. At the end of the dance, Mark led her to their table. His fingers gently brushed her hair away from her face before they sat down. It was a simple gesture, but it felt so intimate Mori held her breath. They were oblivious to the other tables around them. The tenderness of Mark's expression touched Mori deeply.

"Hi ya', Mark, Where ya' been hanging out? Haven't seen you for a spell. Who's the beautiful chick?" A man dressed in a loud plaid shirt, pressed blue jeans, and wearing a large turquoise ring slapped Mark across the shoulders, breaking the special moment.

Mark turned toward the intruder. "Hello, John." He did not introduce Mori.

"Come on. Who's the lady?" He held his hand out to her. "I'm John Cogan, an old classmate of Mark's."

Mori took his hand, but then instead of releasing her hand, he held it.

"Where's Mark been hiding you?"

"Beware, Mori. He's the original coyote," Mark said.

Mori laughed and withdrew her hand. John pulled out a chair and sat down. He helped himself to Mark's beer and some oysters. "Care to dance? This guy isn't worth your time. He's tied up. I'm a better bet."

"Get lost, John. Don't believe a word he says," Mark's words sounded hard.

"Okay, okay. But don't think I'll forget this lady." He disappeared in the crowd.

Mark apologized for the man's interruption.

"Don't bother," Mori said. "He reminds me of my ex-husband."

"Good. That gives me a chance." Mark gave her a look that sent Mori into high gear.

Each time Mark held her in his arms during a dance, his skin felt warm and his feet seemed to sprout wings. She smelled of fresh spring after a hard rain. He dared not look into her eyes, afraid his decision to stay away from any commitment that might lead to another hurt impossible to accept.

Mark was surprised at himself. He never wanted the

music to end as he whirled her dance after dance around the floor. After his wife and son were killed, he'd promised himself that he would never care deeply for anyone again. Just the thought of his son made him feel guilty. He was the one who was supposed to have picked him up on that fatal day. Caring deeply left one too vulnerable to pain. Yet, Mori, who he'd hired to train his horse at Cecile's insistence, was arousing something deep within him. She was becoming very special to him, in spite of his resolve. An excitement of desire resounded through his veins. He was unaware of the jostling crowd, the loud music, or the noisy voices. Words were unnecessary.

The boisterous activity in the bar prevented them from talking, but they didn't need to say anything. Her eyes glowed. Mark felt a warmth and a comfortable trust pass between them. No one else mattered.

Neither of them wanted the night to end. Mark and Mori did not leave the bar until nearly midnight. On the drive home they didn't talk, but Mark drew Mori close to him. She tucked her face against his chest. His heart beat loudly. The defenses he had built up so carefully since the loss of his family were disintegrating. Withdrawing his arm, Mori huddled against the car door. Mark looked at her, puzzled by her action, and concentrated on the road.

"Will you come in for coffee?" Mori asked when they reached her house.

"It's late. Remember, I'm going to be here early

tomorrow." At the door he cupped her chin in his hand. "I had a wonderful time, Mori. One I'll remember." He paused and then kissed her gently. "You are beautiful."

"That's the second time today. You're a flatterer." Mori opened the door to her house.

"Not guilty. See you tomorrow. Good night." His voice hung on the word tomorrow.

Chapter Seven

The graveled road Mori and Mark traveled wound through some of her favorite country. Caught by the brilliance of the rising sun, steep-sided red buttes contrasted sharply with the carpet of short green grasses common to the high plains. Views from the high plateau to the snow-capped peaks swept the land to the west. Much of it belonged to Mark. Mori relaxed and enjoyed the ride.

"We'll soon cross the old Overland Trail route," Mark pointed out several narrow ruts cutting north over prairie grasses and sandstone slabs.

"I know," Mori said. "When I was a kid I'd ride my bike up here to look for arrowheads and hunt for dinosaur tracks. I'd be gone all day."

"Trespassing, huh?"

"Yes. But I never thought about it."

"You had a long bike ride. That must have been thirty miles, at least, from your old home."

"Mm hmm. Once I got my bike, the sky was the limit."

Mark glanced at Mori. "How old were you?"

"About eleven when I first came up here."

"And your parents never cared."

"They didn't know. My bike gave me such freedom. I ran into your grandfather a few times. He'd say to me in a gruff voice, 'What're you doing here? Where's your folks?' I'd gulp and answer that they were on the road."

"That was probably my great uncle instead of grandpa. My uncle ran the ranch."

"He scared me. He looked so fierce on his horse, and he always carried a rifle in a scabbard attached to the side of his saddle. Believe me, I pedaled for all I was worth back to the road."

Mark laughed. "I can picture that. Actually he was very kind. He never married and when he died he left me his half of the ranch."

Surprise registered on Mori's face. "I thought your father left you the ranch."

"His half was divided between my sister, brother, and me. They wanted to sell. I didn't so I traded my stocks and the interest I had in the department store for the ranch. Now they think I didn't pay them enough." Mark sighed.

"Land values have increased in the last several years."

"They forget that. The store has also increased in

value." Mark shrugged his shoulders in resignation. "So, when does Emily get a bike?"

"She has one but it's too small so I'll give her a new one on her birthday. She's far more interested in riding her horse and I know where she is. I might not if she's on her bike."

A smile tugged at the corners of Mark's mouth and his eyes were bright with laughter.

"It isn't funny," Mori said. "So many people live here and so many strangers. It isn't safe."

"You let her go ahead of you while we were riding, remember."

Mori glanced at Mark. "That's different. I was only a short distance away."

"But you couldn't see her."

"True."

"I'm out of line. She's your child. I apologize."

A silence developed between them. Mori watched the road. It curved and twisted around red and pink buttes and through dry arroyos. Clusters of juniper dotted the sides of the draws that contained small springs. Yellow, white, and lavender wild flowers nodded their heads in rhythmic tempo with the breezes that swept across the open spaces.

"You know, it probably wasn't safe around here when you were a kid either. But Emily is entitled to her chance to explore." Mark interrupted her thoughts.

"What would you know? You aren't a parent." The minute Mori made the comment, she was sorry. She glanced toward Mark in time to see the dark shadow that crossed his face.

"Oh, I'm sorry," Mori muttered.

"That's okay. I'm sure I'd be sharing your feelings had my son lived. He'd be ten next week."

Mori caught the sadness and longing in his tone of voice. In the time she had known Mark, he had never mentioned much about his son. Mori made no comment, hoping Mark would say more. An uneasy silence filled the cab of the pickup again.

They began a long descent toward a cluster of buildings next to the river. To slow the truck, Mark shifted into a lower gear. The road switched back several times and then leveled out near barns and corrals. Mark pulled to a stop in front of a large, old log house.

"We've got a couple of hours before breakfast to round up the horses we're taking to the rodeo. The grounds are two miles north of here."

Mark grabbed Mori's overnight case from the pickup and opened the door for her. She followed him to a porch that ran around three sides of the house. The door flew open and a small, strawberry-blond woman came toward them.

"Hi there, Mark. Glad you could make it."

"Hi, Ann." Throwing one arm around her, he introduced her to Mori.

"This is Ann Wood. She and her husband, Tom, manage the ranch. And this is Mori Jordan."

Taking her hand, Ann led Mori into the living room.

"It's nice Mark's brought a woman for a change. I get mighty tired talking ranch business every time he comes. Carry her things up to the guest room. Then get down here for some breakfast."

"Thought I'd have time to help Tom get the horses."

"That can wait." Ann led Mori through the dining room and into the kitchen.

An old Majestic range and a new electric range stood side by side between two doors that led to a pantry and a utility room. Sun streamed through the square window panes. Smells of brewed coffee, mixed with fresh fruit and sourdough pancake batter made Mori's mouth water.

"If you want to wash up, there's a bathroom on the other side of the utility room. Hope you're hungry."

"Famished. I'll be right back and give you some help."

While washing her hands, Mori heard a loud bell clang outside the kitchen door. Returning to the kitchen, Mori was greeted by a red-haired, wiry man not much taller than Ann.

"Hello. I'm Tom. Glad you're coming to the rodeo. We can use some new competitors."

"I'm not competing," Mori exclaimed.

"Mark told us you were an excellent rider. Had me pick you out a horse. He's already paid your entrance fee for the barrel race." Tom hugged Ann.

"I can see by your expression, you're surprised," Ann said.

"Well, yes. I haven't practiced barrel racing for a couple of years."

"Don't worry yourself none. Copper is well-trained. He's got enough heart to take care of the race by himself," Tom pulled out a chair for Mori just as Mark came into the kitchen.

Ann served scrambled eggs, bacon, fried potatoes, pancakes, and coffee. She passed a tray of syrups. "Made them myself from chokecherries, currants, crab apples, and plums. Take your choice. The fruit all comes from the ranch."

Mori poured deep-red chokecherry syrup on her pancakes. "How do you stay so thin eating like this?" she asked.

"Tell you the truth, we don't eat like this every day," Ann answered.

While they passed food around the table, they discussed the events for the day.

"I'm taking my barbecued baked beans and some pies for our share of the potluck," Ann said.

"Got the steers at the rodeo corrals. Merle and Buss and I rounded up about thirty yesterday," Tom said.

"How many coming?" Mark asked between bites of fried potatoes.

"Expect thirty or so competitors, and another sixty family members. Thought you and me could ride over with the horses and Ann and Mori could drive the truck."

The men left early. Mori helped with the dishes. They carried the beans and pies to the truck and packed them in a box.

"Hang on to your teeth. It's a bumpy ride to the rodeo grounds," Ann said as she drove away from the ranch.

At the speed Ann drove, it took but a few minutes to reach the arena. Mori hung onto the dash with both hands to keep from flying out of her seat. By the time they unloaded the food, the morning events were about to start.

The local rodeo ground, built and maintained by the ranchers, met the standards of the best. Chutes were at the north end, bleachers at the south. The arena floor was covered with several inches of soft dirt to prevent injury to participants and animals.

Using a bullhorn, the announcer, Sage Carter, a former professional performer, opened the events precisely at ten. He called the first event of the day.

Ann and Mori straddled the top rung of the corral next to the chutes to watch the calf-roping. Ann clapped her hands continually and shouted cheers or boos as each rider followed the calf from the gate. Once the rope was thrown, the rider dismounted, threw the captured calf on its side, and tied three feet together with "piggin" string. The calf supposedly had to stay tied for six seconds.

"The record's 5.7 seconds," Ann said above the noise of the yelling crowd, the snorting and bellowing of the bulls and steers, the kicking and thumping of the horses in the chutes.

Both Ann and Mori hollered encouragement to Mark and then Tom when they followed their calf across the arena.

Mori liked the steer wrestling that followed the best. With Tom as Mark's hazer to keep the animal on course, Mark pursued the large tan-colored steer from the chute. At the right moment, Mark jumped onto the steer, grabbed it by the horns, stirring up a cloud of dust with his boots as he skidded through the dirt, and wrestled it to the ground so that head and feet pointed in the same direction. Almost afraid to watch the dangerous event, Mori held her breath, hearing the shouts of approval coming from all sides of the arena.

"Hey folks, the record for this event is 2.2 seconds. Mark, here, just did it in 2.4 seconds. How about that for a city-slicker coyote?"

A loud roar erupted. Mark brushed his pants off and, with a broad grin at the spectators, picked up his hat and scrambled toward the fence. Ann lightly punched Mori with her fist, "Hey, he did right well."

Mori shook her head in agreement, glad the event was over with Mark unhurt. Mark climbed the corral rails, brushing Mori's shoulder as he went. Her heart pounded and her stomach seemed to flip at his touch. They faced each other, eyes meeting. Mark gave Mori a masculine grin that sent her pulse racing. Then he was over the fence and back on his mount for the team steer roping event with Tom as a partner. They did very well, finishing in third place.

All too soon, it seemed to Mori, it was time for the barrel-racing event. Mark led Copper to Mori.

"Copper is well-trained for the barrel race," Mark told Mori. "He's a runaround."

From experience Mori believed of the three major turning styles, the run-around, the roll-back, and the front-feet turners, the runaround horse was the best.

"He's been trained to check himself. We've never used spurs on him."

Nodding approval, Mori studied the animal. He was a middle of the road size horse with medium muscles, a slender neck, and a long hip with his hind legs slightly set under him for quick stops and turns. His color—a solid, bright, shiny copper—gleamed in the sunlight.

"He's quick and reliable. A soft cluck just as you come out of the turn helps him get away from the barrel at a faster pace."

Mori petted the horse and talked to him. She moved to the left side to check the cinch before mounting. Once in the saddle, Copper took quick short prancing steps, eager to begin the event. She talked to him and he cocked his ears as though understanding her words.

At the signal Mori got as much speed as possible out of Copper, checking the horse about two lengths away from the first of three barrels arranged in a cloverleaf. She held the reins in her right hand. As Copper went into a stop, Mori took a deep seat, pushed the saddle horn, and turned to look at the barrel. Keeping her body weight over the withers to help the horse arch his body and form a pocket, they spun around the obstacle.

Mori moved into a standing position over Copper's withers as he came out of the turn. She moved up over his withers, never leaning in or out so she would not upset his balance. Quickly she switched the reins into her left hand so it would be next to the barrel during the second turn. Copper increased his speed. Two lengths from the next barrel, Mori checked him and let him drift out a little to form a pocket with his body. She slid him into a run around the turn and then broke him out for the third barrel, putting all her efforts into gaining speed. Copper followed her body signals without a mistake, never slicing the barrel or cutting short by dropping his shoulder into the barrel that could cause serious injury to the rider. A repeat at the third barrel, and Copper, with a burst of speed, headed for the finish. With her body in a standing position, still slightly touching the saddle, Mori assisted the horse. She knew they had gone through the maneuvers flawlessly and in excellent time.

The spectators roared approval. Mori slowed the horse to a walk, petting his neck with her left hand, praising him in cooing tones. When she got off the horse, Mark noticed her controlled smile and the pleasure she felt. Leading the horse to the corral, she tied him. It crossed her mind that Shawna would never be able to compete as she had and it gave her a deep feeling of satisfaction. She gave Copper a treat.

Mark threw his arm around her waist and swung her in a circle. "I'll be surprised if you aren't first," he said.

"I hardly did anything. The horse is the champion," Mori responded. Mark planted a kiss on her forehead before letting her go.

"Don't you ever show emotion?"

Mori laughed.

"Eating time at the end of this. Let's get some coffee. We'll watch but I doubt anyone, even Ann, will come close to your performance." He led Mori by the hand to a table that stood under a temporary awning.

"Hi, Mark." A woman carrying two coffee cups approached Mark from behind the table.

"Hi. See you have some coffee for some thirsty competitors." Mark took the cups from her.

"Nice ride, lady." The woman brushed her hands down the sides of her jeans.

"This is Mori. Elsie." Elsie shook Mori's hand.

After the last event, the crowd queued up to the tables to help themselves to barbecued beef ribs, salads of all kinds, baked beans, vegetables, rolls, and dessert. Mori, Mark, Tom, and Ann sat on the prairie grasses with several other ranch neighbors.

Talk immediately turned to livestock, the price of steers and heifers, irrigation, and hay production. Mori watched Mark with interest.

"You know," Ann whispered to Mori, "Mark's never brought a woman to the ranch before. You must be special."

Mori laughed self-consciously. "Not really. I'm training his horse."

Ann arched her left eyebrow in disbelief. "He's got us to train the horse."

Inwardly, Mori wished Ann's observations were correct. Outwardly, she knew they were not, but then she decided that wasn't entirely true.

Getting to his feet, Mark offered to bring Mori dessert. "What'll it be? Cake, pie?" His gaze met hers. His hands held onto the plate and her hand. The strength she felt sent shivers through her whole being. Her lips parted and her throaty answer broke the silent barrier that seemed to hold them as one for only the moment.

"I'll try the cake," she said.

"Mark, you'd better get dessert for Mori before it's gone."

"Right." He took the plate from Mori and ambled toward the table.

They finished their cake just as Sage Carter announced the first, second, and third place winners of the events. Mark won first place in calf roping. Mori won the barrel race. When the ribbons were presented Mark gave Mori a hug. "Knew you'd be best," he said.

Mori smiled. "This is the most fun I've had in ages."

After the food was packed in cars and trucks, and horses and steers loaded into trailers, the table and awning were taken down. Mark and Tom decided to drive their steers to a nearby ranch pasture while Ann and Mori returned to the house in the truck.

"I'm bushed," Ann commented on the short drive. "A

soak in the tub is what I want. How about you? We'll have time before the men get here."

"Sounds great."

Mori showered in the small bathroom adjoining her room and dressed in faded jeans and blue shirt. She grabbed a sweater before she went to the living room.

A corner stone fireplace two stories high dominated one wall. By its position in front of the windows, Mori assumed it acted as a solar collector during the day and then heated the room at night. From the window she could see the lawn leading to the river and the bluffs and beyond to the snow-covered peaks of the Rawah Mountains.

She turned to study the pictures hanging on the walls. Several were prints by Russell and Remington. Family members decorated the wall above the piano. Two held her interest. One was of Mark on a horse with a baby seated in front of him and the other showed him standing next to a small pony holding reins in his right hand. A blond boy of about four sat on the horse with both hands folded over the saddle horn. She knew the child had to be Mark's when she leaned forward to study it more closely.

In both photographs, the child clutched the saddle horn. He seemed completely relaxed, slouching against Mark in the one photograph, hunched forward in the other. Further inspection of the walls revealed no pictures of Mark's wife with or without the child and that puzzled her.

Mori was concentrating on the pictures so when Ann came up to her she jumped. Then she laughed nervously.

"Didn't mean to startle you," Ann apologized. "Those photos are of Mark and his son when he was two and again when he was six just before he was killed."

"He looks so small. I thought he was younger."

"No." Ann made no other comment.

"He resembles Mark a bit."

"Yes, but he had Denise's eyes and nose." There was another pause and then, "For a long time Mark wouldn't allow us to hang these pictures. Took him a while to get over the death of his family."

"That's understandable."

"Yes. How about something to drink before Mark and Tom get here." She led Mori into the kitchen. "What'll it be?"

"Ice tea if you have some." Mori sat in one of the kitchen chairs and folded her hands in her lap.

"Want some sugar?" Ann asked as she filled the glasses from the sun tea jar.

"No thanks."

"Let's sit on the porch. It'll be cool as soon as the sun goes down."

The women carried their glasses outside and sat down. The sounds of the river carried to the porch and there was the sweet smell of Russian olive in the air.

"How long has Mark's family been dead?" Mori could not restrain her curiosity.

"Let me see. Rob would have been ten in one more week. About four years. He's buried here on the ranch."

"Next to his mother?"

"No. She's buried in town. Never liked the ranch. Wouldn't come out. I only met her a few times. Guess she got bored out here, but Rob loved it." There was a long pause as Ann studied Mori, until Mori felt uncomfortable. "You know you're the first woman Mark's brought here since the accident," Ann repeated herself.

"Oh, that seems unlikely."

"It's true."

"I've heard he's had many women companions since the accident and that he's about to be engaged to Shawna," Mori ventured, hoping that she didn't sound too curious.

"Humph," Ann grunted. "Gossip does get around. I'd be surprised if Mark would want to tie himself up with another lady who doesn't like the ranch. They're friends. The ranch is Mark's love. He's always talkin' about the day he quits his law practice and moves out here."

Mori saw Mark and Tom amble toward the porch. Brushing hats against dusty jeans, they stomped up the wooden porch steps. When Tom reached the porch, he picked up Ann's glass of tea and drank it.

"Hey, that's my tea," Ann protested. Tom stopped her with a kiss. Mark leaned against the porch and glanced at Mori.

"You look fresh as a daisy," he commented.

"The shower I had felt terrific."

"Well, if you'll excuse me, I'll clean up. Can't present myself to the proper advantage smelling like a horse and looking like a hay hand." When he passed Mori, his hand briefly touched her shoulder.

"Hold it," Ann ordered. "Backdoor for the two of you. You aren't going to track up my clean house."

With sheepish grins, the men walked down the steps and around the porch.

"Men," Ann snapped. "Suppose they'll be hungry. Guess I'd better think of something to eat. How about you? Anything sound good?"

Mori laughed. "No! I'm overstuffed from the barbecue. But let me help you."

"Maybe some southwest omelets would do," Ann said. Mori followed her into the kitchen to help whip eggs while Ann chopped green peppers and onions and grated some cheese.

The smells drew the men to the kitchen like cattle to a salt block. A glance at Mark and Mori felt a strange feeling course through her body. The sleeves of his shirt were rolled to his elbows, exposing muscular arms.

Mori caught Mark studying her. Without expression on his face his eyes roamed over her, clearly stating he appreciated what he saw. Mori blushed. Ann interrupted Mark's concentration by placing a platter full of omelets in his hands.

They ate on the porch. Ann, Tom, and Mark discussed the ranch. Mori sat quietly only half-hearing their words, stealing glances at Mark, mesmerized by the cadence of his words. While they talked, they drank several cups of coffee. Mori knew she would never sleep but she didn't mind. As the evening grew colder, she pulled her heavy sweater around her.

"Think you and I'd better clear the table and hit the sack," Ann said to Tom. To Mori she added, "If you need anything let me know."

"Thanks. I think I'm well taken care of." Mori stood to help Ann before going to her room for the night. Filled with a restlessness, she wished Tom and Ann would stay longer so she could remain with Mark.

"No need to help," Ann said. "Might as well go into the living room and sit a spell longer. Still early." Mori inwardly thanked Ann even though she thought she noted a hint of conspiracy in her voice. Mori glanced at Mark.

"Let's go inside." He took her arm and led her to the door. "Sure you don't want some help?"

"Got Tom."

Mark offered Mori a seat next to the window and then sat in a chair across from her. He slouched in the chair, arms dangling loosely over the side, one booted foot crossed over the other. Facing each other, Mori watched Mark and knew she was falling in love.

They sat quietly, listening to the rushing stream heard through the open windows. For a time neither one spoke. Mori stood and walked to a wall containing trophies won by Mark.

"I didn't realize until today you were a rodeo competitor. I thought you were strictly into American Hunter Seat Equitation," Mori's words sounded shaky and low.

Mark came to stand next to her. "When I was young, I took a lot of razing from the men here on the ranch for that so I entered the rodeos to show them I could handle both. My mother thought I was stepping below my 'station in life,' but I liked the competition and here on the ranch I rode Western saddle. My mother insisted I take up English or I never would have."

Mori paused at the photograph of Mark and his son. She felt Mark observing her and she turned to look at him. He said nothing, making Mori uncomfortable and filling her with an odd sense of dismay.

"Ann told me this was your son," she said ignoring a warning voice whispering in her head to say nothing.

Mark returned to the old leather chair he'd been sitting in, a dark shadow masking his face. For several moments his expression was bleak and filled with grief. A tension grew between them. When he spoke, his words were cold and bitter.

"Rob was cheated in life and out of life," his voice broke.

Mori felt his anguish and despair. She wanted to reach out and touch him, to comfort him. Biting her lip, she went to him. Kneeling before him, she took his large hands in her small ones.

"I'm sorry I asked about him. I didn't mean to cause

you such pain. Please forgive me." She took a deep breath, her heart pounding in her ears.

In a gentle voice, he said, "You didn't know. I owe you the apology." His eyes were dark with a faraway look that told the depth of his grief.

Mori did not release his hands. Neither spoke. The clock was the only sound in the room. It was all Mori could do to keep from taking him in her arms to distract him from his remorse.

Chapter Eight

From the tone of Shawna's voice, Mori knew she was angry. As usual she was brusque, demanding, and rude, but the anger puzzled Mori.

"I'll be at your farm around eight. I'm bringing two friends who want to rent horses. I'll ride Strawberry, of course."

"What experience have your friends had with horses?"

"How dare you ask me that."

"I need to know what horses to give them to ride."

"They are experienced riders. Give one of them Mark's horse. I know he won't mind."

"I can't do that."

"What do you mean that you can't?"

"I'd have to have written permission from Mark to let

124

one of your friends ride one of his animals. I don't own the horses, as you know."

"I'll speak to Mark about you. He won't like it."

"Do that."

A loud bang sounded in Mori's ears as Shawna slammed the phone onto the receiver. With a shrug of her shoulders, Mori placed a call to Jake at the barn.

"I know it's early, but Shawna's coming with two friends to ride. Could you bring in Strawberry and Stripe and Misty? Shawna will be here about eight."

"You sure you want Stripe and Misty? They're purty frisky."

"According to Shawna, her friends are experienced riders. I'll come to help you as soon as Emily's on the bus."

"I can manage. No need to hurry."

"Thanks."

After talking to Jake on the phone, Mori fed Emily breakfast, walked her to the bus stop to see her off to school, and then hurried to the barn. Jake acknowledged her presence with a grunt and the two hauled out saddles, blankets, and bridles for the horses. They had just finished when Shawna and her friends arrived.

"I do hope you've provided Cathy and Dara decent horses," she snapped.

"All our horses are decent," Mori retorted angrily. "Before you leave I need you to sign a waiver releasing us of any liability should an injury occur and you can leave a deposit with Cecile," Mori said to Cathy and Dara.

Shawna protested, "This is ridiculous and is wasting our time."

"It's okay. No problem," Dara said. The women walked to the office.

Mori and Jake led the mares out of the barn. Shawna grabbed Strawberry's reins from Mori and mounted.

When the women returned, they talked to the horses they were to ride. As they left the corral Mori watched, relieved that both women handled the animals well. Neither had asked for assistance from Mori, unlike Shawna, who demanded constant help. Mori grimaced when Shawna jerked Strawberry's head impatiently and spurred the horse forward.

"Enjoy your ride," Mori called as they started along the trail.

"We'll be gone most of the morning. We're going to ride to the state park," Shawna said. There was no mistaking the cold hostility in her blue eyes and Mori shuddered involuntarily.

As the women rode out of the corral, Mori heard Cathy say, "I was surprised to hear that you are taking the week off from work. You're so busy, Shawna. How do you find time?"

"I needed a break and then Mark and I are spending much of the time house hunting. I'm going to fly to Los Angeles with him on Wednesday and Thursday to lock up my offer to buy out my business partner. He wants to retire. Mark's going to help me with the legal end of it."

"Will you be back for the Humane Society dance? We'd hoped we could meet at our house before dinner for cocktails," Cathy said.

"Yes."

Their voices faded as they rode out of range of Mori, but she knew that the comments about Mark were made for her benefit. Mori was hurt. On the weekend, Mark seemed to enjoy her company and even intimated he would like a closer relationship. She had taken the bait. *Why,* she asked herself, *am I always the sucker? First Frank snowed me and here I go again.*

She pulled the corral gate closed, disgusted but deeply disappointed too, that she had let her feelings get in the way of reality. Reading another person's intentions had never been one of her strong points. She admitted, though, that she hoped something might come of a relationship with Mark. Obviously that was not going to happen and it left her feeling let down. For a moment she leaned quietly against the fence.

"Need some help over there?" Jake called. There was a note of concern in his voice.

"No. Just reviewing in my mind what needs to be done."

"I'm headed for the hayfield to bring in some bales. We're gettin' kinda low here at the barn."

"Want me to go along?" Mori offered.

"No need. I'll take the pickup. Keys in the ignition?"

Mori searched her pockets. "Guess so. I haven't got them."

Reluctantly, Mori headed for the tackroom to sort out equipment left in disarray from the weekend riders. The more she thought about Shawna's comments, the more her spirits sagged. Inwardly, she had hoped that Mark would ask her to the dance. She would have to get over this. Mark was just another client. Even so, just thinking about him left her with a tight knot in her chest. She had to accept that his helpfulness when he came to the farm was part of his nature, not his way to express special feelings for her.

With only her thoughts to keep her company while she cleaned the tackroom, she unwillingly thought about Frank. When Frank left her, she vowed she would never again fall in love. Frank had swept her off her feet with his attentions and flattery. It didn't take long after their marriage to realize how superficial his attentions were. Frank needed an audience, needed his ego massaged. Her love was not enough. Within two years after they married he was cheating on her with a secretary from his office. When she confronted him, he shrugged his shoulders saying it was nothing more than having friends at work. She wanted to believe him when he said he loved her, but having affairs became a pattern with Frank.

Mori checked the cinch connect straps and flank cinches of the saddles before placing them on the saw-horses. Each time she placed a saddle over the sawhorse she inhaled deeply, relishing the smell of leather and horse.

Jake returned from the pasture with the hay. Mori left the tackroom to help him stack the bales. When they finished she poured them each a cup of coffee. They sat on hay bales and discussed the farm.

"Looks like were goin' to have to call for additional irrigation water if we don't get more rain," Jake commented.

"Sure don't like thinking about a drought," Mori frowned and took a sip of her coffee. "Think we ought to bring in those three mares that are about to foal?"

"I'll get them in 'fore I leave." Jake placed his empty cup on a shelf holding the thermos of coffee. "Back to work."

Mori returned to the tackroom. On the way she caught sight of Shawna's sports car. Mori admitted that Shawna had much more to offer Mark than she did. There was no doubt that Shawna had everything going for her. She was rich, breathlessly beautiful, and very intelligent. Her business acumen put her in the lead among her competitors. She had money and social position and she made the most of it by volunteering for every cause that attracted publicity.

The thought of volunteering and being in the public eye made Mori cringe. She knew she should do more for her community, but she lacked time. It was all she could do to keep up with her business and give Emily the attention she needed.

Well, Shawna, you have nothing to fear from me. You and Mark were friends long before I came on the scene.

Mori knew Shawna and Mark's wife had been friends. Nedra had told Mori that Shawna was the one who helped Mark over his grief.

With saddles in place, Mori picked up the blankets and shook them before putting them over the saddles. She hung bridles and hackamoors under the name plates of the individual horses. Dropping one accidentally caused the curb chain to clank against the bit. Memories of her last night with Frank flooded her mind.

She was in the middle of washing dishes when Frank came into the kitchen.

"It's time for you and the kid to move out," he said in a cocky voice.

The glass Mori held fell to the floor and broke into several pieces. "What?" she asked in disbelief.

"Jen needs a place to live and it would be uncomfortable with you and her under the same roof."

Fire surged through Mori's body. How could he? She'd swallowed her pride, ignored the knowing stares, hoped she could win his love and loyalty when he got the philandering out of his system. Now he was ordering Emily and her out when she should be kicking him into the street.

Through the blur of flowing tears, Mori bent to pick up the pieces of broken glass. She grasped the largest piece and stood up. Shaking the jagged glass at him, she exploded.

"Frank Jordan, you're not bringing one of your cheap women into my house! I've had it with your lying and cheating. You're a disgrace as a husband and father." Her whole body shook as she pointed the broken glass toward the door. "You're out of here. I want you out now."

In less than an hour, he'd gathered his clothes and most of his belongings.

It still rankled her deeply when she recalled his last comments and his nonchalant attitude. "Tell you what. It'll just be awhile. I'll be back. Explain to the kid."

With the last of the tack in place, Mori swept the floor. Now Frank expected to waltz back into her life as though nothing had happened. She snorted in disbelief, suspecting he had some ulterior motive in mind.

Surely Mark was not like Frank. She had thought he was different. Yet, her friends had told her Mark liked to date women for a time and then drop them. He had almost fooled her. So much for Mark and his attentions. She didn't need him. Her commitment was to make her business successful, pay off the money she owed to Cecile and the bank, and make a home for Emily.

The phone beeped. Mori propped the broom in its corner and answered.

"Mori, Steve is on the line and wants to talk to you." Cecile called from the office. "We don't have a sick animal, do we?" Cecile's voice held concern.

"No. I haven't any idea why he's calling."

A press of a button connected Mori and Steve.

"Hello."

"Hi. Steve here. You going to the dance with me? Haven't heard."

"I forgot. Sorry I didn't call. I guess so."

"Good. Pick you up at six on Saturday. We're going to go with Rick and Helen, Nedra and some guy named Sam. Know him?"

"No." Inwardly Mori breathed more easily thinking that her friend's affair with John must be over. She hoped Nedra would not attend a public function with a married man. "I can meet you in town if you'd prefer not to drive out here."

"Don't mind. Got a sick pup so got to hang up." Mori heard the phone click into place.

Finished with the tackroom, Mori mucked out stalls, brushed horses that were in the barn, and then went to her house to shower and change clothes. Four students were coming for lessons at one o'clock, part of a program she had arranged with the college Physical Education Department.

Shawna and her friends returned from their ride shortly before one.

"We had a nice time. I like the horse I rode," one woman said. "She kept me on my toes. Where shall we leave the animals?"

"Tie them to the hitching post. I'll tend to them later."

Shawna stood to one side holding Strawberry's reins in her right hand, waiting for her friends to go to the office to pay for the horses.

"I'll be along in a minute," she called as they walked out of the corral. "Meet me at the car."

When they left, Shawna turned toward Mori. In a tight, controlled voice, she said, "Leave Mark alone. He's mine."

Stunned, Mori stared into Shawna's flashing eyes. "What?"

"You heard me. Stay away from Mark."

For a moment Mori said nothing, knowing she had no claim to Mark's attentions, but Shawna raised her ire. She snapped, "I think that's for Mark to decide."

"He's already decided." Shawna threw the reins at Mori and stomped out of the corral.

Disgusted at her own retort, Mori picked up the reins. *Shawna should have realized I'm not a threat. She didn't need to warn me.* Just the same, disappointment flowed through Mori's veins. It was hard to give up the notion that there had been something special between Mark and her. She sensed a caring and kindness in him that he kept under tight control. She wondered if he considered such emotions in himself a weakness in his character. The sadness in his eyes that Mori noticed so often touched her deeply too.

With resignation, Mori led Strawberry into the barn. To rid herself of her thoughts about Mark she removed Strawberry's saddle and bridle and fed her grain before returning for the other two horses. Activity always helped improve her mental attitude.

The college students arrived on time, filled with enthusiasm. Mori checked out the level of their riding knowledge and gave individual pointers to each girl as they rode around the training ring. One student, Jaia, expressed interest in eventually participating with her own horse in dressage.

Before leaving, she asked, "If my parents will let me bring my horse to school, could I board him here and take lessons from you?"

"It can be arranged, but you'll need to speak with my partner in the office."

After the lesson she asked Jake to take care of the horses and went to meet Emily. The feeling of defeat returned and she buried her emotions by helping Emily with her homework and then fixing them a supper of tacos and salad.

Once Emily was in bed, Mori's spirits sagged again. In her bedroom, she rummaged through her closet for something to wear to the dance coming up on the weekend. It helped her regain a more cheerful outlook.

It had been four years since she had attended any function that required dressing up. She pulled out a cream chiffon knee length dress with a slightly gathered waist, elbow length sleeves, and a V-neck. It would work. Her off-white shoes matched well enough and, since they had not been worn recently, she slipped them on to see if they fit. With their low heels, she knew she wouldn't be taller than Steve. *So much for that.* Before going to sleep she read a mystery.

The week flew for Mori. Warm spring weather brought a renewed interest in recreational riding, keeping Cecile, Jake, and herself busy. On Saturday, Cecile insisted Mori leave early so she would have time to drive Emily to her parents for the weekend.

"I want you to enjoy yourself at the dance. Steve is a nice young man and you need to go out more often," Cecile said.

"You sound like my mother," Mori said.

"Well, if I do, it's because your mother and I agree. Now get along with yourself."

Returning home from her parents' house, Mori showered for a second time that day. With a hair dryer she managed to tame her naturally curly hair into a reasonable style. Her nails were an unsolvable problem. She applied polish but didn't think it helped. When Steve arrived, she was ready.

"Wow! You look great," Steve exclaimed. "You'll be the best-looking gal at the dance."

"Thanks," Mori said.

"You clean up mighty well. We make a handsome couple, if I do say so. Let's go show ourselves."

Mori laughed. Steve reminded her of a cock pheasant - small in stature but showy in his actions.

On the way to town, Mori had to remove Steve's hand from her knee several times. It annoyed her to the point of telling him to take her home but, because she wanted to see Shawna and Mark together, she continued to brush away his hand. His immaturity was one of the traits that made her question his competence as a veterinarian. Finally she told him in no uncertain terms that if he couldn't keep his hands to himself he could turn around and take her home.

"Okay, okay, but a guy's got to try."

They met Nedra, Sam, Rick, and Helen near the entrance to the Marten Hotel.

"Mori, you look stunning," Nedra whispered. "I think we'd be better off if we kept you down on the farm. I'm jealous." She introduced Mori to Sam. "He owns a real estate office too."

"Where have you been hiding, gorgeous?" He shook Mori's hand and then held it for an unreasonable length of time.

"Watch it," Steve said. "She's mine for the night."

Nedra gave Mori a warning glance.

"We're glad you came," Helen said. Rick hugged her.

"You look magnificent," Rick said.

Helen's eyes sparkled with laughter. "Take it easy, love, or I'll be dragging you home where I can keep you out of temptation's way."

Since Steve was on the board of directors of the pet shelter as well as a sponsor of the affair and the guest speaker, Mori and he were seated at the head table. Mori's attention was on the crowd. She glanced around the banquet room hunting for Shawna and Mark. If she saw them together, it would help her forget her interest in Mark.

Minutes before the dinner was served, Shawna and

Mark arrived at the head table and were seated next to Mori and Steve. "Hello. You look out of this world," Mark said softly.

Her response was cool and Mark frowned, puzzled by her unfriendliness. Shawna acknowledged Mori's presence with a sugary-sweet smile. Then she distracted Mark by calling his attention to the size of the crowd. Uneasy with Mark sitting next to her, Mori turned to talk with Steve, but was surprised at Mark's apparent interest in pet care.

When the food came, Mark whispered, "Can't say this food is the best."

Mori smiled half-heartedly in agreement. She barely touched her banquet-style roast beef and mashed potatoes.

After dinner as MC, Mark introduced Steve.

"Our featured speaker is Dr. Steve Dodge. Most of you already know that he is one of our veterinarians who is actively working to check the overpopulation of pets and the problems that occur when no one wants the baby animals."

To Mori, Mark's voice became a drone even though she focused her attention on him as did everyone in the room. When Mark finished he returned to his seat, his eyes meeting Mori's. Not until Steve began speaking did he turn away from her.

"I'm pleased to see such a large turn out. As you know we are using the proceeds from this dinner and the dance that follows to raise money to set up clinics for the neutering of dogs and cats. Every year we put hundreds of sad-eyed, unwanted, but loveable pets to death because no one wants them. This must end. Our program will make neutering of animals affordable to everyone and bring this tragic practice to a halt."

Listening to Steve, Mori admitted he was a good speaker. The sincerity in his voice and words impressed her. Mori hoped that the function would bring results. An animal lover, she had seen too many cats and dogs abandoned by owners, left to roam the countryside until killed, starved, or picked up and delivered to the Humane Society shelter. Cecile and she had done that enough times. It always made them angry. Mori observed the reactions of the crowd to Steve's words.

"And so, friends of dumb animals and the county Humane Society, I hope you will find it in your hearts to promote our animal control program. Leave the breeding of dogs and cats to legitimate kennels. Encourage others to neuter their animals and we'll be able to lick a major problem. We can put an end to this insidious cruelty to the animals we love."

The applause was long and loud and Mori felt certain the efforts of the pet society would be successful.

Shawna dragged Mark away from the head table immediately after the talk. Steve and Mori joined their friends.

"Steve's talk was convincing," Helen said.

"As usual," Nedra commented. Uninterested in further discussion about the speech, Nedra headed for the ladies lounge with Helen and Mori. She flopped down in an overstuffed chair and crossed her long, well-formed legs.

"I've had a week to end all weeks." She jangled the many gold bracelets that covered her arms. "I'm beat but I love it. I've sold four houses including a mansion in Claredon Hills to Shawna."

Combing her hair, Mori paused and looked into the mirror at Nedra's reflection. Nedra noticed her surprised reaction.

"I'm puzzled," Nedra continued. "Shawna bought the house, not Mark. I tried to get a listing on his house, but he doesn't want to sell. Now, how are they going to live in two places that aren't half a mile apart? Maybe there is hope for you yet, Mori." Nedra smiled.

Helen shrugged her shoulders. "Who can understand? With the money they have, maybe they want two houses and plan to use them for different purposes."

Nedra forced a cough. "Come on. You can't believe that."

Finished with touching up their makeup, the women left the lounge.

Mori enjoyed dancing and never lacked for partners. It surprised her to realize how much she had missed dancing. Steve, who lacked rhythm and only knew a few steps, attempted two dances with her but each time she had to lead him.

"I think I'd better leave you to other partners," Steve admitted. "I'm a miserable dancer."

"I don't mind," Mori said.

Halfway through the evening, Mark interrupted her dance with Steve, who was trying to keep up with Mori but was obviously uncomfortable.

Holding her away from him, Mark whistled quietly through his lips. "You are the most beautiful woman here you must know."

"I know flattery when I hear it," she chuckled. "I became well-versed in it with my ex."

"I'm serious." He pulled Mori close to him. She could feel the warmth of his breath on her ear and smell his aftershave lotion. In his arms she was aware of his strength and the hardness of his body. She was embarrassed and horrified to have a welling up of desire for him. Just this afternoon, she had let go of the idea there could be anything between Mark and her. She tried to push away from him, but he pressed her harder against him. A deep turbulence inside her caused her to tremble. He released her and looked into her face. His eyes were clouded and unreadable.

Had she been able to read his thoughts she would have realized his desire for her was held in tight control. He wanted to take Mori from the dance to his home to be with her and no one else.

Damn, Shawna, he thought. Since his wife's death, Shawna had been manipulating him. He understood Shawna and knew she liked possessions. Over time he had become a possession to her. She quickly forgot her possessions until something or someone threatened to take them and then she drew them around her like King Midas collected his stash of gold around him. He hadn't minded her possessiveness in the past. It had freed him from more than one relationship he did not care to continue. But this time was different. His feelings for Mori were troubling to him.

Since meeting her and being around Emily, he found himself thinking he would like a family. For years, he had avoided being around children. Seeing families together was too painful. But Emily had wrapped him around her finger and he was almost willing to admit that he was falling in love with Mori.

Although Shawna and he had discussed marriage they knew it would be a convenience and nothing more. They always backed away. As long as Shawna could control him and possess his time when she desired, she was satisfied.

To curb his growing attraction for Mori, he asked, "What's between you and Steve?"

"That's no concern of yours," Mori said, thinking of Shawna. The tension she felt eased.

"He's not your type."

"How would you know?" she asked.

"I know." Holding her gently, he pulled her against him and whirled her around to the music.

"So you have a better selection."

Mark wanted to answer that he was better, but didn't. He left the words hanging in a void in his mind. Holding her close, he led her around the dance floor enjoying the feel of her in his arms. He touched her face against his and he felt his stomach tighten with desire.

To distract her emotions, she said, "I've heard you are committed."

Before Mark could answer in surprise at the comment, the music ended and Mori was claimed by Steve who took her to their table. Shawna's dance partner led her to Mark and they returned to their table. Mark felt a deep disappointment that he had to leave Mori.

"That was an interesting bit of interplay," Shawna said. "She is a pretty little thing but so obviously out of her class. I wonder what Steve sees in her."

Mark said nothing, controlling his desire to defend Mori.

At Mori's table, Nedra smiled curiously at Mori, an expression of teasing jealousy touching the corners of her mouth. Mori sat down filled with regret that the dance was over.

Rick and Helen stood to dance. Sam and Steve excused themselves.

"Well, well, that was quite a show," Nedra said. "I doubt any of us missed the actions between you and Mark. You should have seen Shawna. If looks could kill, you'd be dead."

Mori blushed. "We were only dancing."

"That is the understatement of the evening."

Chapter Nine

In the weeks that followed the dance, Steve called Mori several times to ask her out but she refused. No calls came from Mark, and he did not come to the farm to ride Sunny Day, nor did Shawna come for lessons. Mori searched the society section of the city newspapers but found no mention of Mark and Shawna together. She did read with interest Shawna's negotiations to acquire a competing real estate management firm, and she noted Mark won a case involving a false arrest. Mori assumed the two were busy.

In as discrete a way as possible, Mori attempted to gain information from Nedra over lunch. On a slow day at the farm, Mori drove to town to buy supplemental feed for the colts and met Nedra in a small delicatessen next to her office and across the street from the county court-house.

"What did you think of Sam?" Nedra asked. "Isn't he a doll? And he isn't even married. Never has been. Imagine that. We've been dating ever since the dance."

"He seemed nice enough," Mori answered. "I thought, though, that he seemed, well, sort of feminine."

"Oh, come on. Your trouble is that you want every man to be like Frank—a chunk of muscles."

"You couldn't be more wrong. All Frank has is body."

"And personality."

"That's about as deep as a blank sheet of paper. Anyway, I don't want to talk about him or mention him for that matter." Mori paused. "Be careful, Nedra, with Sam."

Nedra laughed and shrugged her shoulders. "When's Frank taking Emily for the summer? School's out soon."

"He isn't. He says he's too busy, but I haven't told Emily because I know she'll be disappointed."

Mori glanced out the window and across the street. Her heart did a flip as she watched Mark come down the stairs of the courthouse and across the street toward the delicatessen. He was engrossed in conversation with a beautiful, professionally dressed woman. Mori looked at her five-year-old pant suit and felt self-conscious about her appearance. When Mark and the woman walked into the restaurant, the color drained from Mori's face.

"What's wrong with you, Mori?" Nedra asked.

"Nothing." Mori coughed.

Nedra turned and looked. A smile spread across her face. "So that's it. Here comes lover boy."

"Nedra!"

"Nedra, my foot. You've got the hots for Mark just like the rest of us."

"Who's with him?" Mori couldn't resist asking.

"That's Louise Graves, an assistant district attorney."

"What does Shawna think of her?"

"Nothing. There was a rumor, but Shawna came out on top. Now Mark and Louise are working out something on a protected witness case the D.A.'s office is handling. Mark is involved as part of the defense team representing the person involved."

As Mark entered the deli, he caught sight of Mori. He smiled, sending shivers down her spine. Mori acted as casual as she could, putting her hands under the table to conceal their trembling.

Mark stopped at their table and looked at Mori. "Hello, Mori, Nedra." His intense gaze held Mori's. "How's my horse?" The sensuality in his voice caused Mori's blood to pulsate to her face.

"She's doing well. I've put a saddle on her a few times. She doesn't mind it, but the first time I attempted to use the saddle, she upset my balance. She has settled down." Her words sounded husky and unnatural.

"I'll be out in a few more days. How about joining me for a ride to the park? I'll give you a call as soon as I can make it, and I could use a two-hour guided trip."

Mori giggled to relieve the tension she felt. "You need a guided trip like I need sour milk."

"I'm serious."

"Cecile handles our reservations. If you call her, she can give you our scheduled rides. There may be others going out at the same time."

"That won't do. I want a private ride." Mark paused. "How's Steve?"

"I wouldn't know. I haven't had any sick horses since the dance." The smugness in Mark's expression told her he was pleased and it surprised Mori. She wanted him to show he was glad she hadn't seen Steve since that night.

Louise sat at a table near Helen and Mori, but Mark seemed reluctant to leave. When he did, he touched Mori's shoulder, glancing into her face and holding her attention with his penetrating stare. Mori smiled and turned toward Nedra.

When Mark left, Nedra said in a whisper, "I'm so envious. What's your secret?"

Mori ignored Nedra's question, biting into her sandwich so hard she bit her tongue.

"Hah! I knew it," Nedra remarked emphatically.

"Mark is going to marry Shawna. Remember you're the one who told me."

"Well, there's always a chance they may change their minds. They've done so in the past and, if you play it right, you might come out on top. I can help."

Mori gave Nedra a disgusted look. "Eat your lunch."

During the remainder of the meal, Mori felt uncomfortable, certain Mark was watching her. It took effort to keep from turning toward him. Nedra was aware of her discomfort and giggled more than once in spite of her outwardly sophisticated appearance. With relief, Mori finished her lunch and left the delicatessen with Nedra without turning to say good-bye to Mark.

Glancing at her watch, Nedra said, "I have another hour before my next appointment. Larson's Department Store is having a fabulous end of the season sale. Why don't we shop?"

"I should get back to the farm. Besides, I don't have any money for clothes."

"The bargains are stupendous. I buy many of my clothes at their sales."

"Nedra, you've got to be joking. You always look like you've just modeled for the latest fashion magazine."

"I have to dress well, but I can't afford to pay full price for all the clothes I need. Come with me. You might find something."

"I guess I can take another half hour or so."

Together, the two walked the few blocks to old downtown and the department store owned by Mark's family. It took up one full block.

"Did you know Mark's wife, Denise?" Mori asked. "I don't remember her from school."

"She went to private schools in the East and was also older than we are by five or six years." By the tone of Nedra's voice Mori sensed that the age difference seemed to give her some satisfaction.

"So you didn't know her either."

"Oh, I knew her. I sold them the house Mark lives in now."

They waited at a corner for the light to change. Cars whirred past them, filling the air with exhaust fumes that made Mori cough.

After crossing the street, Mori asked, "What was she like?"

"Beautiful. Denise looked a lot like Shawna. The two of them were inseparable friends and, I think, they were snobs of the first order. Although I belong to the country club, I was never worthy of so much as a hello from either one of them, and I even sold Denise's condo when she married Mark. She knew me."

Mori caught an expression of resentment that furrowed Nedra's forehead and a wave of darkness that spread over her face. Mori wondered if Nedra blamed her unfortunate childhood as the reason Denise snubbed her. She knew Nedra was sensitive to anyone who gave her the impression they were better than she.

"Denise and Shawna played golf, bridge, tennis, and traveled together before Denise died in that horrid accident."

"What happened?"

"I forgot that you were away when it happened, so you don't know the details." Nedra's voice dropped to a whisper. "It was rumored Denise was drunk. Been drinking that afternoon at the club. She picked Rob up at his school, and on the way home ran a light and smashed into a telephone pole. Killed both of them instantly. Neither wore a seatbelt. It absolutely devastated Mark. Shawna was right there to offer him her shoulder to lean on."

Pausing in the middle of the block, Mori stared at Nedra in disbelief. Nedra defended herself. "It's true. It's what I heard."

"But that's a nasty rumor to spread about."

"I'm not the one who started it. Some members at the club said she was drunk. Mark hushed the whole thing with Shawna's help."

"Perhaps it's better she died. I can imagine how she would have felt if she'd lived and her son had died." There was compassion and sympathy in Mori's voice.

"Who knows?" Nedra shrugged her shoulders.

They entered the first floor of Larson's. The store was filled with eager sale shoppers. One look at them, their shoving and jostling to get waited on, and Mori was ready to walk out, but Nedra grabbed her arm and led her toward the escalator.

"Women's wear is on the second floor and don't waste your sympathy on Denise. She couldn't stand the little boy. Never wanted to be pregnant."

"That's a terrible thing to say."

"It's true."

At the second floor, Nedra and Mori wound their way through hosiery, lingerie, sleep wear, and coats to get to the dress department. Nedra zeroed in on a rack of suits and blouses and quickly ran through the garments until she came to a blue jacket with a matching blue plaid skirt.

"What do you think? Like this?" Nedra asked.

"Looks like you."

"If I buy it, I can put it away until next fall," Nedra held the jacket up to her shoulders.

"Try it on."

"Look at this, Mori. This is you." Nedra removed a gray suit with a paisley lavender, gray, and white blouse. "Try it on. It is a size six."

"I can't buy anything. And where would I wear it?"

"It's seventy percent off. Come on. You can't afford not to buy it if it fits."

In amazement, Mori watched Nedra try on, select, or discard dresses, suits, and jackets like a whirlwind. When Nedra finished, she purchased more clothes than Mori expected she could wear in three years. In spite of prodding by Nedra, Mori resisted the suit, but she did find two cotton shirts she could wear on the farm.

In the weeks that followed, Mori hoped Mark would call but he didn't. As the days passed, she became angry, not at Mark, but at her vulnerability. She decided she was the world's biggest fool where men were concerned. It seemed when a man paid attention to her, she thought they wanted more than friendship.

When Mori looked back on her first date with Frank, it had been the same thing. She'd thought Frank wanted a relationship. He hadn't, but she'd pushed him, and her sorority sisters encouraged the relationship. Frank was popular, good-looking, and a football player. Everyone she knew envied her. Her situation with Mark seemed too similar. There was no doubt in her mind that she was one person who was better off single. Her luck with men was bad.

Mori kept occupied with her business and Emily, who in her restlessness for school to end, drove Mori to distraction. When Mori told Emily she couldn't visit Frank during the summer, Emily became cranky and naughty.

"You don't want me to go," Emily accused Mori. "You don't like Daddy and you won't let him take me."

"That isn't true," she said. "Your father is establishing a new sales territory and isn't going to be home long enough to have you for a visit."

"I won't get to see my other grandma and grandpa either," Emily wailed.

"Perhaps we can work something out," Mori said. "I can't promise, but I'll try. I know they love you and they'll be disappointed so I'll call them"

"When?"

"We'll try tonight."

Arrangements were made for Emily to go to her Nebraska grandparents for a visit near the end of July. In fact, when Mori called, they were delighted to hear from her. She knew they loved Emily dearly and were as distressed as her own parents when Frank divorced her.

At the end of the school year, Mori enrolled Emily for

two weeks at a friend's summer dude ranch. During the summer, her friend took children for two-week periods. They went camping, swimming, horseback riding, and hiking. She also gave each child a colt to train.

"Leaving the colt at the end of the two weeks is hard on the kids, but they learn from it," her friend said.

While Emily was at camp, Mori and Cecile were busy with day rides and lessons. Both acted as guides and instructors. After one long morning ride, Mori received a call from Mark.

"How's my horse?" he asked.

"She's doing fine."

"She's probably as wild as a longhorn, it's been so long since I've been out to see her," he said.

"No. I've worked with her on a regular basis. She's got a lot of energy. Don't want her to forget her training."

"Thanks. I'm coming out today to ride. Want to join me?"

"I can't. We have two women coming during their lunch hour for a ride and some visitors from the convention center this afternoon and I have a late afternoon lesson."

"What time are you finished?"

"Late, probably not until five or six," Mori replied.

"Well, the days are long. Maybe I can change your mind." He hung up before Mori could protest.

Whenever Mori had a lull during the remainder of her busy day, she glanced at her watch, anticipating Mark's arrival. Her spirits were high and her feet seemed to float across the ground. She hoped she would have time to change her clothes and fix her hair before he arrived, but he was at the corral early.

Mori's heart skipped a beat when she saw him leaning against the pole fence. Dressed in faded jeans and shirt, he looked sensational. Mori gulped to control her flustered feelings before greeting him.

"Need some help?" Mark offered. He swung one long leg over the top pole and then the other and dropped to the ground.

Mori noticed her women riders ogling Mark. They stood waiting for Mori to introduce them to Mark, but instead, she led them to the gate and opened it.

"Will you please check out at the office," Mori said.

The two women thanked Mori but kept their eyes on Mark, pausing for a few seconds, trying to gain his attention. Then they turned and walked to the office.

"It's been a long time," Mori said. "Sunny Day may not remember you."

"Too long. What do you want to do with these horses?"

"I've got another lesson so I'll use them."

Disappointment flickered across Mark's face. "So, I've got to ride alone? Thought I was going to get a guided trip."

Mori laughed. "You did? You know as well as I that you don't need a guided ride. I'd feel guilty charging you. Besides, Cecile has to run to town and Jake is leaving early, so I have to stick around here 'til we close or until Cecile returns."

"I think you at least owe it to me to go to dinner," he persisted.

Mori started to protest.

"Emily too."

"Emily is spending the next two weeks at the Three Bar Ranch."

"Well, no excuses. When is your lesson finished?"

"It'll take about an hour.

"I'll be back. Think Sunny's ready to ride?"

"Yes, I think you should give her a try. She's old enough. She may be uncomfortable at first so go easy on her. She's in her stall." Mori led Mark into the barn and down the aisle. "You know where to find a saddle."

As Mark rode away from the barn, Mori's student arrived. Though she was tired from the activities of the day, Mori greeted her student, Renee, with enthusiasm. Renee, who attended the city college, was quick to pick up suggestions to improve her horsemanship. She possessed "horse sense" understanding without being told what to expect, sitting the saddle in close and relaxed contact with the horse. Renee never ran or shouted around the stable, and she checked the horse and the fitting of equipment before she mounted. Mori watched Renee put the horse through a canter around the track, keeping the horse under control with the aid of her legs. When she came around the ring, Mori directed her to go again.

"Keep your eyes closed this time to get the feel of the horse and his lead. It's a good way to learn the movements of your mount."

"Okay." Renee rode around the track a second time, her body absorbing the shocks and thrusts of the horse in a relaxed and balanced manner without apparent effort.

At the end of the lesson, Mori complimented the rider. "Your hand action is much better. In fact, your control appeared very light."

"Thanks, I love to ride. You know, the whole time I was growing up in the middle of Los Angeles I wanted a horse. My friends were into swimming. I went swimming, but I dreamed about having a horse."

"A lot of girls feel that way," Mori said. "I know I did."

"Maybe I'll have my own horse yet."

When the lesson ended Renee led the horse to his stall, removed his saddle and bridle, and put on his halter. Then she brushed and curried the horse, obviously hating to leave. After she finished she led the horse out to pasture.

"See you in a couple of days."

As the girl got into her car, another one drove into the farm. Mori wondered who could be coming so late. Leaning against the gate she waited for the new arrival to get out of the car.

"Oh no!" Mori groaned. "Frank. What does he want?" She closed the gate and walked toward him.

When Mark returned to the corral a few minutes later with his mount, he heard a loud male voice. The horse flicked her ears nervously. Mark dismounted and walked to the end of the barn to check out the voice. In front of the office he saw Mori and a man he recognized immediately as Frank. Shoulders slumped forward, hands clasped together in front of her face, Mori gave Mark the uncomfortable feeling that she needed help. Frank towered over Mori.

Knowing Mori was alone, Mark draped the mare's reins over a pole in the corral, hurriedly opened the gate, and walked quickly to the office, noticing each person's posture as he approached them. For the first time he realized how vulnerable Mori was when left alone at the farm, and he didn't like it.

Neither Mori nor Frank saw Mark approach until he was almost upon them. An expression of surprise and then relief flooded Mori's features.

"Hello, Mark. How was your ride?" Mori asked.

Mark heard the tremor in her voice. "Fine." He stared at Mori and then at Frank.

"You remember Mark?" Mori asked.

In a voice filled with sarcasm, Frank answered, "Oh yeah, loverboy himself."

Frank's sneer angered Mark, but he controlled his annoyance. He held out his hand, managing to sound affable even though his mouth showed a distinct hardness. "Hello."

"Frank is just leaving," Mori said. Mark did not miss the disgust in her brown eyes. He restrained the urge to reach out and draw her to him.

Frank made no comment, his features unfriendly, trying to mask the annoyance he conveyed in his voice.

"I didn't know I was leaving. I was going to spend

time here with Emily, but since she's at some camp, I'll hang around until she comes home. I thought I'd bunk with Mori and keep her company."

"There are excellent motels in town," Mark said. His voice was civil in spite of his feelings of anger. He noticed Frank's eyebrows draw together in an unpleasant frown, and he felt a challenge.

Mark quickly surveyed Frank as an opponent. He was almost as tall and heavier, but there was a softness and flabbiness around his middle. Mark closed his fingers into the palms of his hands and his lips thinned, revealing the irritation he felt. For a moment, Frank took measure of Mark.

Mori broke the tension. "I've arranged for Emily to visit your parents in July, and there are places in town for you to spend the night."

Frank regarded Mori with his mouth opened in surprise. Mark noticed a weakness in Frank's soft, flabby jaws.

"I told ya' I couldn't have her visit me this year."

"She's staying with your parents. They wanted to see her," she said.

An uncertainty crept into Frank's expression. "Well, that'll give me a chance to visit Emily when I'm home."

"So you have no need to wait around until camp is over," Mori continued. Her hands, clutched behind her back, twisted nervously, and Mark sensed her inner anxiety. A surge of deep affection and a need to protect her filled him.

"Guess so." Frank paused. A disturbing expression replaced his smoldering look. In a voice that sent a cold warning through Mark, Frank continued, "Damn shame you're wasting my support payments on some stupid camp. You never could manage finances, and I doubt you can manage Emily. Maybe I'll look into your actions and behavior." His voice left no doubt in Mark's mind the threat to Emily and Mori. He noticed the color drain from Mori's face.

"I'm not interested in your opinions," Mori sighed with weariness in her voice. "So why don't you leave, and I'll get back to work." An uncertainty crept into her eyes.

Mark fought to restrain himself from putting a fist into Frank's mouth. Frank turned, and with an insolent swing of his shoulders and arms, ambled toward his sports car and opened the door. Before climbing into his seat, he looked directly at Mori. His mouth twisted with cynicism as he spat out, "Take care." To Mark it was more like a threat than a farewell.

Frank turned the ignition. He pumped his foot hard on and off the gas pedal; the engine roared as though sending a warning. Frank backed out and then shot straight toward Mori and Mark. Mark grabbed Mori to the side just as Frank spun the car away from them. His laughter rang through the air, leaving Mark with feelings of uneasiness.

Chapter Ten

The noise of the roaring engine faded into the air and finally became nothingness. Only then did Mori's body end its shaking. Mark continued to hold her in his protective grip. A quietness rolled around them. All Mark heard was his own thumping heartbeat. Mori remained in his arms. He was reluctant to let her go.

"Are you okay?" he asked gently.

She stirred and pushed herself to a sitting position, brushing dirt from her pants. "I think so. You?"

"I'm fine," Mark said as he faced her. He noticed her concerned expression. Remembering the whole scene angered him. Mark continued to hold her. He ground his teeth together as he did when he was furious.

"He could have killed you," Mark said. "You never told me he was dangerous."

"He really isn't," Mori avoided Mark's eyes.

"Believe me, the man's dangerous," Mark said.

"I don't think he'd ever hurt me. He just has to have his way and when he can't, he can be a bully or even cruel sometimes. But I can't believe he ever intended to hit us. He's probably enjoying his antics and thinking he gave us a good scare."

"Well, he did give us a scare. You were shaking pretty bad. What does he want anyway? Why is he all of a sudden showing his face and making threats?"

"He says he wants me back, wants to move in with Emily and me, wants us to resume our marriage. I told him absolutely not. Frank only wants what he can't have. When he gets it, he doesn't want it anymore."

Mark still was not convinced that Frank wasn't a threat, but it relieved his mind that Mori refused Frank. "My opinion, for what it's worth, is that he has something in mind." A feeling of happiness swirled inside him, but it was quickly replaced by fear for Mori's safety when he heard a car approaching. With lightning speed he jerked Mori into the office.

"Stay here," he commanded. He slammed the door as he left the office and then positioned himself next to it, ankles crossed, ready to face Frank should he return to the farm.

Cecile drove into the yard and parked her truck. Mark relaxed and went toward her. Mori came out of the office to follow him.

"Good heavens, who was that man racing along our

road? He created so much dust he blinded me. I'm calling the patrol," Cecile said, looking at Mark. "And what's wrong with you? You look like you're ready to take on an army."

"That was Frank. He just tried to run down Mori," Mark growled between clenched teeth. "It's a good thing I was here. I didn't know he was such a skunk."

"What do you mean, he just tried to run down Mori? Cecile asked, the color draining from her suntanned face. Mark quickly described the incident.

Cecile faced Mori, hands on hips. "Why haven't you told me how dangerous Frank is? If anything happened to you, I don't know what I'd do."

"Mark is making a mountain out of the situation. Frank's just in one of his spoiled little kid moods, pulling a practical joke on me, trying to get me to change my mind." Her face was wan and colorless, defying the certainty of her words.

"That was no practical joke," Mark said. "He deliberately tried to run you down." Mark turned to Cecile and continued. "I don't think Mori and Emily should be left here alone."

"You may be right. Let's go inside. I'd like more details."

Mark opened the office door, and Cecile and Mori entered. Cecile poured them each a cup of strong day-old coffee and waited to hear what happened.

Seemingly without taking a breath, Mark related Frank's actions. The more he talked, the quieter Cecile became, holding her coffee cup tightly in her hands as though afraid she might drop it. Mori paced the room, now and again interrupting Mark to restate her position that Frank was trying to force her to change her mind.

The irony of defending Frank's actions left an unpleasant feeling in Mori. *He's like bad graffiti scribbled in my mind,* Mori thought. *He's after something else.* Mori set her cup down. *He wants my share of the farm, but why?* The thought chilled her.

"He also threatened to take Emily from her. It wasn't so much what he said, but how he said it," Mark continued. "I wouldn't put anything past the guy. He's dangerous."

Mori stopped pacing around the room. Fear replaced her feeling of anger. "He can try, but I won't allow it. He doesn't even want Emily to visit him for the summer. He's too busy. If he's too busy for a visit, then think what would happen to Emily if he got her all the time." A cry of despair escaped from deep within Mori's throat as well as fear.

Mark put an arm around her shoulders, and Cecile took her hands.

"He won't get Emily," Mark hissed.

"We'll never allow it," Cecile emphasized each word, her lips pressed into a firm stubborn line.

Mori realized she had to pacify Mark and Cecile before the two marched out of the office to go find Frank. She chuckled as she pictured them, fists drawn, ready to accost Frank.

"Mori, it isn't funny," Cecile said.

"I can just imagine the two of you taking on Frank, that's all. Besides I know Frank, and I can handle him." Color returned to her face and she breathed more easily with a growing sense of confidence.

"Perhaps we should ask for a restraining order," Cecile suggested.

"That's hard to do unless we can prove he is a danger and, even then, they don't always work," Mark said.

In her own mind, Mori could think of nothing she'd like more than never to see Frank again, but she knew Emily loved her father. For her Mori would never talk against Frank or keep her from seeing him. She believed to do so would undermine Emily's security and her belief in herself.

"Hey, we've talked enough about Frank," Mori interrupted, "but for the record, Frank believes everyone in the world is gutless but himself. If he shoves someone a little, that person will back down. Next time that person will do exactly what Frank wants when he shows up. He usually telegraphs his action. He tilts his head slightly to one side, runs his finger over his right eyebrow, and then looks at you with a menacing stare. His expression says he's planning more drastic action. He did that before he got into his car." The mental picture of Frank made Mori frown. "He just can't shove me anymore."

No matter what Mori said, Mark was convinced Frank was a danger to her. With the help of Cecile, he determined Mori would no longer be left alone.

"Hey, you two, it's getting past dinner. How about joining me for some supper?" Cecile put her cup in the sink and pulled the plug from the coffeemaker.

"I'm really not very hungry," Mori said. "I think I'll finish up at the corral and shower and go to bed."

"I was hoping to take Mori to dinner at the Sushi Den. That is, if she likes Japanese food." He looked at Mori. "Why don't the three of us go together?"

Cecile grinned, her blue eyes sparkling. "I think you'd have to drag me back to town. You two go and enjoy yourselves. I'll change clothes and finish chores."

Mori started to protest, but Cecile held up her hand to silence her. "It'll do you good to get away from here, but when you get back, spend the night with me, Mori. Okay?"

"I don't feel right about leaving the work for Cecile. I really can't go," Mori said.

"I'll help you," Mark said. "It shouldn't take us long."

"Well, okay," Cecile said. "As soon as I'm changed I'll be down to help."

Cecile locked the office while Mori and Mark headed for the barn.

"I really don't think I'd better go to dinner," Mori said. She led Sunny Day toward the barn. "I'll have to shower and change clothes before I go with you, and I know I don't want Cecile to face Frank should he return."

"So you are concerned? Go ahead. I'll take care of Sunny and the other horses. What needs doing?" He took hold of Sunny's halter. "We'll see if we can convince Cecile."

"I can't do that. You pay me to board your horse. That's my job."

"Don't argue. Sunny is my horse, and after being inside all day, this is recreation to me." *And taking you out is too,* Mark thought.

Mark convinced Mori after some discussion. He unsaddled Sunny Day, brushed her, and led her to the pasture. Hoisting two saddles at once, he carried them to the tackroom and put them away. When the equipment was in place, he checked the stalls for cleanliness and grabbed a shovel to pick up the pile of horse biscuits that needed removing. Cecile arrived in time to check the gates and feed. In spite of Mark's pleading, Cecile refused to join them for dinner. By the time the two finished chores, Mori was dressed.

"That didn't take you long. You look very nice," Mark whistled. "Now you've got to wait at my house while I shower and change. Hope you don't mind. We've got to call for reservations too."

"You can call from here." Mori handed Mark her cell phone.

"We'll wait. You can call while I change."

Mori had been to the ranch, but she had never been in his home in the southern part of the city. She was curious to see that part of his life. On the drive to town they talked very little, Frank's situation dangling between them like an iron ball.

Mark drove to red sandstone gates that led into Grand Mesa Estates, one of the most exclusive subdivisions in the area. Mori glanced from one side of the street to the other, admiring the beauty of the homes.

At the end of a cul-de-sac, Mark steered his four-wheel drive up a lane bordered by Rocky Mountain junipers and stopped in front of a large two-storied adobe house. He climbed out and opened the door for Mori. She stood for a moment, studying the tan, Spanish-styled home with black wrought-iron at the windows and the double black-painted doors.

"Come in. I'll hurry. It's getting late." He led Mori into a spacious hall with black tiled floor and white walls. A stairway curved upstairs to a balcony below a large crystal chandelier that hung from the ceiling. Her shoes clacked across the tile as she followed Mark into a living room with white carpet, black leather furniture, glass and ebony tables and lamps.

"The telephone is next to the wall on the table by the door, and the phone number is in the leather book next to it. Can I take your jacket?"

"No, thanks, I'll keep it on. It's cool tonight."

"Want something to drink?"

"A Coke would be okay."

"Diet or regular?"

"Diet."

Mark went to the wet bar, filled a glass with ice and the drink, and set it on the coffee table for her. "Make yourself at home." He bounded out of the room and up the stairs.

When he left, Mori called for reservations. Filled with restlessness, she picked up her Coke and wandered around the room.

Neither the house nor the room conformed to Mori's perception of Mark. It was too sterile, too cold. Even the impressionistic paintings hanging on the white walls did not add warmth to the room.

She went to the window. The backyard backed up to a golf course, and she watched two golfers in the lingering daylight take turns hitting the ball. When they finished, they climbed into their cart and drove away.

Turning around, Mori caught sight of a toy box pushed into a corner that was full of trucks and cars. On the floor beside it sat a yellow tractor. The toys looked as though they had not been touched in years, but they gave life to the otherwise perfectly coordinated room. Mori studied the toys. She was surprised Mark had kept them. Even the tractor on the floor obviously had not been moved for years, evidenced by the dust around it.

Mori searched for photographs of Mark's family. There were none. Then feeling like a snoop, she sat down on the black sofa. The cushions were soft and she felt herself relax. Putting her glass on the coffee table, she leaned back and closed her eyes.

She heard Mark come into the room.

"You were fast," Mori commented. "I almost fell asleep."

"Didn't want to keep you waiting."

At the Sushi Den, the waitress dressed in Japanese kimono led Mark and Mori to a small room enclosed with silk screens. The elegant restaurant had a calm, serene beauty. Soft music and lovely flower arrangements enhanced the Japanese mood.

At the entrance to the room, Mori and Mark removed their shoes and put on slippers, then sat on cushions and folded their legs under a low table. Their feet touched. Mori took a deep unsteady breath to subdue the jolt of excitement that ran up her leg. She quickly crossed one leg under the other. Mark's smile was seductive, and she blushed as exciting pulses beat in her chest. She reminded herself she was almost thirty-one, too old to indulge in such nonsensical feelings. Mori ran her hand over her hair, a gesture that had irritated Frank. She folded her hands in her lap to regain her composure.

A young woman brought them a teapot, fine china cups, and a menu.

"I'll return shortly for your order." Her voice was melodious and soft in keeping with the tranquility of the restaurant.

"Everything they serve is guaranteed fresh," Mark commented as he picked up his menu. "What would you like?"

"I don't know. You choose. I've never been here before."

"How about an appetizer of yahitou? Or we could have salad, white rice, and miso soup."

"I'd like that," Mori answered. She savored the sound of his voice that sent ripples of awareness through her body.

Mark smiled, his gaze on her, not the menu. The tremor in her voice touched him, and he knew he could watch her forever, never becoming bored with her reserve or the inner beauty she possessed. She wasn't sophisticated or worldly or devious, and she didn't play games like Shawna. He admired her honesty. She was forthright and gutsy.

"We have choices of tempura with teriyaki chicken or shrimp or trout or beef with sashimi." His voice sounded thick, unsteady to his ears. His heart thrummed loudly in his ears and he had the illogical sensation that he was falling in love. The feeling of being in love had been buried for so many years he wasn't certain he was ready to acknowledge it, afraid of the feeling and the possible loss he might experience. He could never live through such trauma again.

"I'll try tempura with shrimp."

"I think I'll order beef. The tempura ice cream is special. Want to have that for dessert?"

Mori agreed with a nod of her head. As she poured hot tea into their cups, her hand shook. The waitress returned and took their orders.

"There'll be a short wait. Everything is prepared at your table while you watch. Would you care for some wine?" the waitress said.

Mori said no. Mark ordered saki.

"Have you ever believed that in this world two people meet and recognize they've met someone who can make them complete in every way, that they're part of you?" Mark asked. His voice was husky and deep.

At first she did not answer. His words startled her, leaving her with a loss. When she did answer, her words were thoughtful.

"I don't know."

"I never did . . . not until recently." The tone of his voice held a tinge of wonderment.

"I suppose I believe in fate, a kind of destiny, at least about many things." Looking into Mark's face, Mori was struck by the extraordinary blue of his eyes.

His expression was serious and quiet. "Maybe love is just a dream, a romantic ideal. Still I'm beginning to believe in it." He shook his head as though he couldn't comprehend his own words. A melancholy frown creased his brow.

"You really think there are two special people meant just for each other?" Mori's expression was one of surprise. "I guess I believed that when I fell in love with Frank, or thought I did. Then I learned that feelings are different among individuals, and I lost my idealism." Until now, she thought, unwilling to divulge such a deep feeling to Mark. She was afraid he might misinterpret her, especially with the strong feelings of desire held just beneath the surface of her uneasy composure.

"I never had that belief before now. When I married Denise it was because it was expected of me. I thought it didn't matter, that we could live together in harmony, understanding and whatever. Everyone thought we were the perfect couple, and I fell into the idea." Mark paused, a look of bewilderment registered in his eyes. "Was I in for a surprise. When I look back, I know we were selfish, both concerned about our own individuality, our freedom to go our own way. I must admit, we occupied space on friendly terms."

Mori sipped her tea, wanting to hear more but afraid to say anything that might discourage him from continuing. She liked the intimacy developing between them. They sat silently looking at one another.

"Only after Rob was born at the end of our first year of marriage did I consider someone else. Denise resented Rob, didn't want to bother with him, so I took care of him." He smiled. "He was as sweet as they came."

Mori felt an inexplicable sadness watching him. She reached across the table and put her hand over his. He looked at her, and she read the deep hurt within his soul.

"I want to believe," he said.

"I want that too," Mori answered in a soft voice. Her words surprised her. Mark cupped Mori's face in his hands.

"I think you are the other part of me," he said.

Mori felt her head spin and her mind swirl in confused

delight. Her wildest secret dream that she refused to admit left her dazed, filled with warmth that surged through her veins. The tenderness in Mark's expression made her heart thump loudly in her ears. She could barely control her joy as her defenses melted away. To break the magnetism of feelings that frightened her and to subdue the rioting within her mind, Mori turned away from Mark's penetrating gaze. She needed a moment to reorient her thoughts. With control, she poured each of them tea, in an attempt to stop the rioting of her heart. Neither said anything, but she felt Mark watching her, and she heard him breathe deeply as though catching hold of his emotions too.

The waitress arrived with salad and miso soup. Mori was relieved that there was something concrete to fill their time, enabling her to suppress her pounding heart. She tried to relax.

Mark picked up his chopstick to eat his salad. Mori's usual reserve returned and the tension within her eased, but Mark continued to watch her movements and her expression. She realized that the attraction she felt for him was evolving into a need. She wanted him near her, to touch her, and to hold her, to help her when she needed it.

Mori picked up her chopsticks and struggled to pick up her food. Mark reached across the table to show her how to hold them between her fingers. When he took hold of her hand, waves of electricity shot through her. Mori resisted looking into his eyes as she focused on the task. Even so, her hands seemed detached from her body, refusing to follow Mark's directions. Mark smiled.

"You must think I'm the worst student you've ever had. You'd better let me struggle and eat your own food." Her voice came out in a whisper.

Mark shook his head. Before letting go of Mori's hand, he ran his finger along her cheek. Mori stiffen under his touch and stopped. "I'll give these sticks another try."

"If you want, the waitress will bring us forks and spoons," Mark said as Mori continued to lose almost every morsel she tried to get to her mouth.

"No. I'm a determined individual. I'll keep trying."

The rice came and Mori managed to push most of it into her mouth by holding the dish under her chin. She ate the shrimp with her fingers. "This is delicious. Want to try some?" Mori asked.

Mark admired Mori's spirit, her willingness to take on a horse business, her gentleness with Emily. He contrasted her with Denise and then Shawna and wondered what he had seen in either one of them. In many ways Shawna and Denise had similar characteristics. Denise was an alcoholic, Shawna was not, but he suspected Shawna encouraged Denise's drinking.

Before marrying Denise, he'd thought she was the most provocative woman he'd met, but he knew he had never loved her. Even now he laughed cynically at his gullibility.

"Why the laugh?" Mori broke into his thoughts.

He smiled. "Nothing. I'm amused at your persistence in eating with those chopsticks."

"Well, I'm in an authentic Japanese restaurant."

"They bring spoons with dessert."

Mori giggled. "Probably a good idea. Otherwise the ice cream will melt and I'll end up drinking it."

Mark was intently aware of Mori's body, her breathing, her gestures. Even the way she held her chopsticks delighted him.

After eating the tempura ice cream, Mori glanced at her watch.

"I'd better have you take me home. I've got to get up early. We have a lot to do before my first student arrives."

"I'd like the evening to last forever," Mark said.

"It's been nice." A smile flickered at the corners of her mouth and then vanished as she regarded Mark with a sudden cautiousness. Her desire for Mark, her disturbing longing for him frightened her. She wanted and needed him. Her feelings alarmed her, and her heart seemed to fill her throat. To pull herself away from him, she stood up and walked to the sliding silk screen door.

Before she could leave the room, Mark took her arm and turned her around to face him. He kissed her. It felt right, and Mori slid her arms around his neck. Their bodies melted together, and she could feel Mark's strength as he ran his hands down her back, drawing her closer to him. At first, Mori relaxed with the intoxication from the shared moment. She uttered a low sigh and heard Mark groan from deep within his throat. It sent an explosion of desire like a warm breeze from her ear to her toes.

Mark held her closer to him. She felt his breath on her neck and the heaving of his chest.

Then her fear of falling in love again asserted itself in her mind and she pulled away from him. Frank came into her mind, his smoothness when they went together, and his complete change after they were married. It frightened her. How could she know if Mark might not be the same way?

Mark looked puzzled, but released her. She wanted him more than seemed possible, but she could not let go of her mistrust.

Chapter Eleven

Lights blazed in the corral, at the office, and in Cecile's home. It alarmed Mori as Mark drove into the farm yard. Before Mark pulled to a stop, Mori was out of his car and running toward the barn, passing Steve's truck on the way. Not taking time to open the gate, she pulled her skirt above her knees and crawled between the corral posts.

The corral was empty but she heard voices coming from the barn. Mori entered through the door and found Cecile, Jake, and Steve. In an effort to suppress her gasp of horror at what she saw, Mori bit the back of her hand. She turned to try to stop Mark from following her into the barn, but she was too late. Mark saw Sunny Day and the shock engulfed his face.

Cecile and Jake, who stood on each side of the mare,

176

held her head between them trying to steady her. Steve bent over the horse's left leg, beads of sweat dripping down his cheeks. At his feet, his medicine case stood open. Bloody instruments laid side by side in a tray filled with antiseptic.

Steve looked up at Mark. "Sorry, old man, but I'm afraid you're gonna have to put your mare down."

Without speaking, Mark stooped next to Steve to look at the mare's left hind leg. A deep groove exposed a mangled mess of muscle, tendon, and bone. The tendon appeared partially severed.

"She hasn't a chance in a blue moon of getting back close to normal," Steve said. "You haven't much choice."

Tears stung Mori's eyes and wet her cheeks as she watched Mark probe the wound with gentle hands. The love he had for the animal was written on his face and it touched Mori deeply. Agreeing with Steve that the horse would need to be put to rest, Mori held her breath as she waited for Mark's decision.

Without hesitating Mark said, "No. I'll keep her alive, give her a chance. If nothing else, I'll use her as a breeding mare."

Steve shook his head in disbelief. "You're crazy man. She'll never make it. Never."

"She'll come out of it. She's got will and her progeny will be quality stock," Mark's voice carried determination. "She's an excellent mare. I won't put her down."

Mori pet the soft velvet nose of the horse. "Yes, you're a fine lady," she said to the mare.

Jake hung his head as though embarrassed to witness the emotions emanating from Mark's voice as he talked quietly to the mare, assuring her he would do all he could to save her. Nodding his head at Mori relayed the doubts Jake had about the decision Mark made.

Cecile looked at Mori and indicated that she thought the decision was not wise. Her eyes expressed the misery she felt. With the back of her hand, Cecile attempted to wipe away the moisture in the corners of her eyes.

Mori knew Sunny Day's bloodlines were outstanding. She had been sired by and foaled by two aristocratic purebred Arabians. She was a proud animal with a high carriage and graceful, elegant movements and she moved with special exuberance. Even in pain she held herself erect and there was a splendor in her bearing. Keeping her alive could mean inexorable suffering and could prove futile in the end.

Mori agreed with the others that they were correct in their reaction to Mark's plan. The horse should be put down, but inwardly she wanted to give the horse a chance and was relieved by Mark's decision. Mark and she could nurse Sunny Day back to health. With her turned in short ears, big wide-set eyes, and deep sorrel color, she was too beautiful to put down.

"How'd it happen?" Mark asked in a quiet voice.

"She apparently laid down near the gate between the corral and the pasture to roll in the dirt. Her back leg must have got caught in the gate under the bottom rail. At least that's where the flesh and blood is," Jake answered, his voice sounding deep and unnatural. "Just sawed her leg back and forth to free herself like she was caught in a trap." His words made painfully clear the panic the horse must have felt.

"I found her and got her to her feet," Cecile said. "I was sick to my stomach when I saw what happened. Somehow I got her into the stall. I gave her some first aid and then I woke Jake for help and called Steve." Cecile paused, trying to control the tremor in her voice. "What a freak accident. I can't believe this happened."

"If we're gonna save her I guess I'd better get her bandaged." Steve rummaged through his kit for disinfectant, antiseptic, and bandages. Carefully, with Mark's assistance, Steve cleaned the wound a second time before applying the bandages. Sunny Day quivered with the applications in severe pain but she stood like a rock seeming to understand the care being taken on her behalf. When he finished, he gave her a shot of antibiotics.

"I'll check in tomorrow morning and see how she's doing," Steve said when he finished. He went to the barn faucet and ran water over his hands. "You understand, she's gonna take a lot of TLC. You prepared to get out here morning and night, lawyer boy, for the next several weeks, maybe months?" Steve looked directly at Mark. "Or you gonna leave it up to Mori and Cecile? They already got more than they can handle."

His questions came as an insult to Mark, who snarled his answer, "I know what's involved. I've been around animals most of my life. Seems you've forgotten."

"Well, folks, I'll show you what's needed just to be on the safe side. Now keep her quiet. Give her these antibiotics to keep infection down." Steve poured several pills into a blue envelope, wrote directions, and handed them to Mori. "I'll give her an injection now, and again tomorrow, and then you start these pills."

Mark bristled, irritated that Steve ignored him, but he said nothing. He took Sunny Day's halter from Cecile and carefully led the mare to her stall. She limped badly to keep from moving the injured leg and Jake walked next to the horse to help her with her balance.

"Really think Mark should put that horse down. The mare is unlikely to ever move her rear leg forward normally. In the end I'll need to put her down." Steve talked more to himself than to Cecile and Mori.

"Mark wants to give Sunny a chance. I've got to go along with him, and I'm sure Cecile agrees." Mori said. Cecile nodded her head.

"Okay." Steve shrugged, picked up his medicine case, and headed out of the barn. "See you in the morning."

Mori walked with Steve to his van. "You're negative, I know, about this, but it's important to Mark and to me that the horse be given a chance. I'll do anything you tell me."

Steve climbed into his van. Before closing his door and turning on the engine, Steve looked at Mori. "You got something going on with high and mighty in there?" He pointed toward the barn.

"That's my business," Mori said.

"Just wondering. He's not for you. Hate to see you get hurt. Now you and me, we're a good fit."

"What would you know," Mori was tempted to say but she let his comments pass.

"See you in the morning around eight. Fact is, I'll be making several calls if that mare's going to make it."

Steve started his truck and Mori returned to the barn where Mark still lingered beside Sunny Day. She felt guilty about the injury to the animal.

"If I'd been home and tended to my nightly rounds, this never would have happened. I'm really sorry. You must have a low opinion of us after this accident," Mori said when she entered Sunny Day's stall.

"Don't blame yourself. Who knows what time this occurred? And I don't have a low opinion. This is one of those freak accidents that sometimes happen. Remember I'm the one who asked you to dinner. No one is to blame."

"He's right," Cecile cut in.

But we've got to check out our gate system so we don't have a repeat of this," Mori said. "We'll help all we can to bring Sunny around. Guess she'll show her grit and just what kind of animal she is."

"If you don't mind, I'll spend the night here," Mark said.

"Not at all. Stay at my house," Cecile offered.

"No. I'll bed down here. Got a sleeping bag in my car and a change of clothes."

"We'll leave the office open for you. Call me if you need anything," Mori said.

She walked with Mark to his car, where he pulled out his sleeping bag and a change of clothes. Mori said good-night but felt reluctant to leave as she continued toward her house. Once inside she surveyed the damage she had done to her hose, shoes, and dress. Her nylons were beyond repair, her shoes were stained with blood and her skirt was torn where she had caught it on the fence. "So much for these," she mumbled. She rolled them into a bundle to dispose of them.

Instead of getting into her pajamas, she decided to make coffee for Mark and take it to him. While the coffee perked, she put on jeans, shirt, and boots. The coffee was ready by the time she was dressed. She poured it into a thermos, put on a light jacket, and returned to the barn.

The black night sky was filled with thousands of stars. A cool breeze rustled the leaves of the cottonwoods muting the songs of the crickets and cicadas and the sweet smell of new cut alfalfa filled the air, but nothing helped to reduce the guilt she felt about the accident.

She entered the barn, quietly determined to leave if she found Mark sleeping but he was sitting on a hay bale near Sunny Day's stall. Mori paused at the door to study Mark's expression. She read sorrow in the way he sat and had to curb her desire to comfort him. After all, he had a reputation of manipulating women and then dumping them, didn't he? She coughed lightly to attract his attention.

"Thought you might be awake and would like some coffee," she said.

"Thanks. I would. I could use some company too."

Mori sat next to him. She poured the coffee and handed him a cup. "I'm glad you're giving Sunny Day a chance, though we both know it's a long shot."

Mark agreed. "My dad would have thought I'm crazy to waste my time and money on her. He would have had her down without a second thought. He never understood my love for horses."

"Well, times change. Today injured animals have a much better chance. You've done the right thing. I'll help all I can."

Mark put an arm around Mori's shoulder and hugged her. "I appreciate that."

Mori sat still wanting Mark to continue holding her but, at the same time, on guard against her feelings. Removing his arm, Mark clasped the cup of coffee in both hands and held it between his knees. He seemed to remove himself from her, lost in his thoughts. Mori knew she should leave the thermos for Mark and return to her house, but she wanted to stay next to him. Warmth flowed through her veins and ended in a flutter in her stomach. She shook her head to clear her mind of the effect Mark was causing. It had taken her too long to recover from the devastation she'd felt after her divorce to fall in love with another man. She wasn't going to let her emotions get in her way a second time.

"I'd better be going," she said. "You probably want to get some sleep before morning."

"Don't go." His voice was almost a whisper. "I need company even if I am acting like a nerd."

"Under the circumstances, I'd act the same." She took a sip of coffee.

"I have to admit I'm keeping the horse alive for selfish reasons. I can't seem to deal with death like I once did— a sort of so what attitude, we all die eventually. Life is more than that to me now. I guess it's for Rob."

And Denise too, Mori thought, *the wife you've never stopped longing for, the one whose memory gets in the way, keeping you from finding someone else. The name of the woman you rarely mention. At least you've spoken Rob's name.*

Hardly breathing, Mori waited for Mark to say more, but again there was only the sound of a horse wheezing and an occasional stomping of a hoof from the stall of a mare about to foal. When the thermos was empty, Mori stood. "Come for breakfast."

"Thanks, but I've got to get to town early. I don't want to wake you."

"You won't. I'm always up by five."

"Well, if it's no trouble." Mark stood. He took Mori's hand in his and drew her to him, putting her hands around his waist. Then he tightened his arms around her. She responded to his kiss, feeling the warmth of his lips, and ran her hands up his back and along his strong neck as she yielded to him. Waves of pleasure built inside Mori as she felt herself carried away by the moment. Delightful shivers ran down her spine. The warmth of Mark's lips tantalized her and she savored the feel of him and the scent of his aftershave.

Mark's kiss lengthened. His heart beat rapidly and his breath came from deep within him as he tightened his hold, pressing Mori closer to him. A moan escaped Mark's throat as he reluctantly released his hold. He softly stroked Mori's ear.

Mori opened her eyes and saw Mark studying her. His expression was sad.

"I'm sorry this happened to Sunny," she said.

Mark leaned against Sunny Day's stall and watched her leave. In a daze Mori walked to her house under a dark sky filled with millions of silver stars.

In the weeks that followed Mark arrived at dawn every day and cleaned Sunny Day's injury before reapplying bandages. After each work day, he checked her again and began moving the limb to keep her from becoming stiff. It became a daily routine to pick away the scabs and clean the pus before applying healing antiseptic and new bandages.

Emily came home from camp. Upon Mark's arrival in the afternoon, Emily, Punch, and Witch tagged behind him to the barn where Emily sat outside the stall to watch him and offer encouragement. Not only did the horse bond to Mark, but so did Emily. Mori watched with interest as Emily became his assistant.

Mori usually greeted Mark when he arrived in the morning. After tending the horse, they often had coffee and sometimes breakfast before he headed to his office or the courthouse.

During Sunny Day's treatment, the mare stood still, never struggling or trying to kick Mark. He had a special touch with the mare's treatment. Gradually the swelling went down and Mark began leading the horse around the corral. Mori knew she would miss Mark tremendously when the horse no longer needed his attentions. She didn't like to think about it and put it out of her mind.

Shawna also made her appearance each evening shortly after Mark's arrival, supposedly to ride. Mori wondered if it was more to keep an eye on Mark. She kept her distance when Shawna was present but observed the sickening look on Shawna's face when Mark worked on the mare's wound. Mori overheard Shawna say more than once, "I just don't know why you don't either put the horse to sleep or let Mori take care of the animal. You are paying her to do such work, or you could take her to the vet hospital."

Patiently, Mark responded, "It's my horse. She trusts me. Sunny is a real fighter and we're becoming very close. She knows I'm here to help her and she'd probably feel betrayed if I abandoned her care to someone else."

"Honestly, Mark, you talk as though she's human. It's ridiculous coming from a man of your intelligence. I'm getting tired of playing second fiddle to a horse. I thought we had more than friendship." Her nostrils flared in disgust.

Emily usually stood in the background and tended to the injured animal when Shawna was around. This time she walked toward Mark as Shawna stomped off. She looked up at Mark and said, "Good riddance. She's pretty stupid about animals."

Mark's eyes met Emily's serious ones. His own twinkled with amusement. Shawna returned with her handbag dropped over her shoulder and glared at Mark and Emily. "Not only does your horse get your attention, but so does that child."

"She's my helper. We make a good team, don't we, Emily?"

Shawna rolled her eyes and said, "This is too much. Well, at least stop by this evening." Her tone was soft, an attempt at velvet. "Looks like you're about finished here."

"I'll see, but Sunny still needs some treatment. It may be late when I finish up."

"Don't disappoint me. I'll be expecting you even if it's late. You've been late before and it was not a problem." Shawna whirled around and walked out of the barn, and Mark returned to his task of nursing Sunny Day.

It was past eight thirty when Mark left the farm and Mori wondered if Shawna got her wish.

Several days later, Shawna arrived at the farm ahead of Mark and sought out Mori, who was helping Emily with Traveler.

"I'd like a word with you," Shawna said. "Alone."

"Emily, let Traveler out with his mother and go find Cecile."

"Why? We just got started. I don't want to."

"We'll do this later, I promise, Emily."

"Okay." Emily took her time hoping to annoy Shawna, while Mori waited patiently without comment.

"She's rude, so typical of a single parent child," Shawna said. "Your ex thinks he would do much better bringing her up."

Mori arched her eyebrow in surprise. So Shawna knows Frank. "Emily is not rude," she bristled, but still managed to control her anger. "Strawberry is in the south pasture. Jake can get her for you. I'm sure you've come to ride, and she does need to be ridden."

"I'm not here to ride. You know how fruitless it is to try to save that mare. I want you to convince Mark to put that stupid horse of his to sleep. It's taking too much time from his practice and his social obligations."

"Hmm." Mori barely looked at the demanding woman.

Shawna glared at Mori. "Mark is throwing time and money away on that beast. Surely you have enough common sense to realize that. Oh, but of course, you want Mark here morning and night. You fool. You poor woman. It won't do you much good to fall for him. The moment that horse recovers or dies, Mark won't have time to come out here."

Mori remained close-lipped, gripping the rein of a yearling's halter tightly, holding it close to the filly's jaw. The young horse tugged restlessly against her.

"The mare is recovering nicely. She won't need bandaging twice a day. Mark is the one who must decide when he no longer needs to care for Sunny," Mori answered.

Shawna shook her head in disbelief and agitation. "You are as asinine about horses as he is." Their conversation ended abruptly with Mark's arrival.

"Going to ride, Shawna?" Mark asked. He walked to the barn.

"Well, yes, if you'll go with me." Shawna's voice sounded possessive. "Mori can doctor your horse. You need to get away. You deserve it. It'll be good for you." She snapped her fingers at Mori. "Don't just stand there. We need our horses saddled. Mark doesn't have time to waste." Shawna put an arm through Mark's to stop him but he removed it gently.

"I'd like a ride but you'll have to go alone. Strawberry does need exercise, but I've got to change Sunny's dressings and then go to town for a meeting."

"Very well. I'll stop by your house tonight after your meeting. I'll call before I come over."

"It'll be too late."

"Mark, dear, it's never too late for us." To Mori she said, "If you'll get Strawberry, I'll ride around the track a few times."

A few days later, Shawna stopped coming to the farm which left Mori with a feeling of relief. Then Shawna called Cecile and asked that Mori ride Strawberry. "My new business is taking my time, but I do want Strawberry ridden until Mark and I can ride together again."

Mark continued his evening sojourn to treat Sunny Day. Little by little it became natural for him to stay for supper.

As the weeks went by Mark often called to offer to bring pizza or fried chicken or Vietnamese. Sometimes Mori, Mark, and Emily rode horses after Sunny Day's treatment. Usually they ate on the deck and talked about the farm, her debts, and her desire to pay them as soon as possible. He responded about his thoughts of eventually moving to his ranch and giving up his practice.

Once Emily discovered that Mark told wonderful stories, she implored him to tell her one before she went to bed. The stories always focused on a lesson of life or some positive value and involved Emily as the main character. Mori watched with fascination the developing friendship between Mark and Emily.

Oftentimes when the story was ended, Mark remained to talk with Mori about his horse's progress. "I think the girl is going to make it and walk without a limp."

"It's that TLC she's getting from you."

"Not just me. All of us." His voice was matter of fact.

Mark settled next to Mori on the sofa and eased his arm over the back of the sofa; his hand rested on Mori's shoulder. She stiffened at his touch and her heart thundered so loudly, she was certain Mark heard it. Afraid he might know of her reaction, she got quickly to her feet.

"I'll make us some ice tea before you leave. It's warm tonight."

"I hadn't noticed. I'll give you a hand." Mark followed Mori to the kitchen.

While she took glasses from the cupboard, Mark got tea and ice cubes from the refrigerator. "I'm getting to be a regular around here." He took spoons from the drawer.

She paused to stare at him. His gaze stopped her with its electricity. She laughed nervously to subdue the heat that spiraled through her veins.

Mark left the tea pitcher on the counter and stepped close to her, so close she felt his breath when he said, "You're a special woman."

Mori blinked in surprise. "How can you say that when you're engaged to Shawna?"

"Where did you hear that gossip? Shawna and I are not engaged." His voice sounded incredulous.

"From just about everyone including Shawna."

"How can you believe that? Surely you can see Shawna's not the type of woman one marries."

"Well, what type of woman is she?" Mori stammered. "She hangs on you and sweet talks you every chance she gets. I've heard the 'come by Mark, even if it's late, don't disappoint me.' " Mori's words came out sassy and deprecating.

"Mori," Mark seemed exasperated. "I thought you were better at reading people." He paused before he said, "I know what I want." He picked up his jacket and stomped out, leaving Mori completely perplexed.

Chapter Twelve

Disgusted with himself, Mark gunned his four-wheel drive along the dirt road that led to the blacktop. The echo of love distracted him, becoming more than an echo. He wanted to tell Mori he loved her, but could not overcome his reservations about committing himself to another woman. His marriage hurt him still, but Mori possessed none of the characteristics of Denise which led to so much of his pain.

Fueled by her feelings of insecurity, Denise constantly complained. That manifested into actions that were often vindictive and mean. To bolster her self-esteem, she involved herself in one affair after another that Mark refused to acknowledge. When things fell apart for her, she came back to him and promised to give up drinking and stay with him. He had believed her.

At first Mark had been surprised at her low opinion of herself. She was one of the most beautiful women he had known and she was often mistaken by strangers as some celebrity. She was selfish, self-centered and, in the end, an alcoholic. It was her alcoholism that caused the death of precious son, Rob. If he had picked him up as he usually did, Rob would be alive. Trusting his relationship with Mori was affected by Rob and prevented him from admitting his love for her and he knew it.

He remembered the day of the accident as if it was yesterday. It was Shawna who made the initial call to him. Her words rang in his mind.

"Mark, are you with someone?"

"No."

"Be prepared for a call from the police."

"What do you mean?"

"I don't want to tell you. I'll be over shortly."

Mark shivered involuntarily at the panic he felt when Shawna hung up. It was nothing compared to the moment the police came to the door. He could still hear the officer's apologetic words. He wanted them to stop, but they kept coming and coming until the full impact of the terrible automobile accident echoed over and over in his mind. His beloved son was dead, killed instantly with his mother who had skidded into a concrete barrier.

Never again would he hug the little son who greeted him with a galloping leap at the end of each day. Never again would he hear, "Read it again, Daddy." The read-it-again book was the *Jungle Book*, dog-eared and worn from his own childhood. Mark and his son shared the love of Mowgli, the man-cub in the story, his friend, the bossy panther, Bagheera and Baloo, the fun-loving gray bear. In so many ways Rob was like the brave and adventurous young Mowgli.

He was brave when his mother screeched at him for bringing his toys into the living room, for accidentally spilling a few drops of milk, for asking questions over and over. He created his own adventures in his make-believe play. His plastic horse became a wild mustang one day, rodeo bronc another, and a race horse the next.

Mark continued to live with the reality of that awful day. He had to go on, but healing would never be complete. The empty hole would remain until his death. And his regrets. How long would they haunt him? Why had he stayed in marriage to a woman who resented her own flesh and blood? Fear. That was it. Fear that she would take Rob away from him, as she threatened.

"Mark, baby," she had said in sarcastic words, "you know no judge will take a son away from his mother. You'll lose custody. You've seen it happen in your business."

The most painful regret involved the day of the accident. He was scheduled to pick up Rob from his special school that day. A client needed him to work past the scheduled time. It was going to be a hardship, the client said, to make another appointment. So Mark had acquiesced and had reluctantly called Denise to make the stop for Rob. She had sounded pretty steady on the phone, even though she was miffed about having to leave her social engagement early. If only he had put Rob first that day and picked him up as originally planned. Why oh why had he let his work interfere?

The self-blame ate at him relentlessly. If he thought about it for only a moment, despair dragged him to the pits. Accelerating on an open stretch of road he opened all the windows. The rushing air current surged against ears and face. His eyes burned from the blast. If only it would carry his grief to oblivion.

Mark pulled into his driveway. The empty, dark house echoed his brooding mood. Once inside the garage he sat in his vehicle, unwilling to enter his house. When Mori had been there, the lonely emptiness had been filled by the essence of her warmth. He longed for her presence now, but there was this chasm between them, a kind of tug of war.

He climbed the stairs to his bedroom, despair and regret still clawing at him. At loose ends, he turned on his television to catch the late night news. Not a word made sense to him as his focus centered on the woman who tugged at his heart. And little Emily. She was a spunky little girl who plunked at his heartstrings. Was she too old to read the *Jungle Book*, he wondered?

A smile touched his lips and he shook his head thinking that Mori actually believed Shawna and he were engaged. True, he admitted, Shawna and he had an off-and-on relationship and had considered living together once. Some major obstacle by one or the other of them always prevented it. Probably, he thought, because they knew they would not be happy together.

Before he had met Mori, he believed he'd never form a lasting attachment again. He felt different since meeting her. And Emily made him forget his pain, his feeling of loneliness without Rob. For the first time in years, he could enjoy a child without anger.

Mark tossed restlessly, anxious for daylight to arrive. He was out of bed at dawn. He made coffee and called Mori. He wanted to spend time with her at the ranch. Perhaps he could share his feeling in the place he considered home.

"I have to be at court early and I have some briefs to review before I go so I'm not going to come out tonight," Mark spoke to Mori over the phone.

"Okay. I'll give Sunny some exercise."

"Thanks. I hate to miss her workout and you. You most." Her image came to his mind and excitement swept through him.

He heard Mori catch her breath. Mark continued, "I'd like you to go to the ranch with me this weekend. I'm planning to take Sunny Day and see how she does on a longer ride now that her leg is healed. I could use your help."

"I don't know. Emily is to go to my parents on Friday night and I have to drive her. I'm sure you'll want to leave early and I can only spend the day."

"Could you take her early? If not, bring her to the ranch." He tried to sound casual.

"My parents and Emily would be disappointed if I don't take her for a visit. I'll try and get away. I'm sure Cecile won't mind."

"Can I drive her?"

"No, but thanks anyway."

As Mark put down the telephone his stomach felt tied in knots and his emotions were about to run out of control.

Because of his court trial, Mark couldn't get out to the farm but once the remainder of the week. He missed Mori terribly and time seemed to drag as he waited for the weekend. Saturday he picked up Mori and helped her with the chores before loading Sunny Day and Midnight into the trailer. They stopped for breakfast at an old hotel that had been a stage stop in the 1870s. The floor slanted badly and Mori and Mark slid in opposite directions most of the meal. They laughed hilariously every time they looked at one another.

"We'd better give up on this," Mark said. "My coffee seems determined to slide to the floor."

Mori smiled. "I agree, this is a fun old building and the food is good."

Mark stood and held Mori's chair. She lost her balance and fell against him. His arms encircled her waist as he helped her recover. Mori's giggle sent waves of rapture through him. His gaze locked with hers and they forgot the other customers around them. Slowly Mori turned away from him removing his arms from her waist.

"I think I can stand." Her voice trembled as she pushed away from him.

"I'd better pay for our breakfast," he said recognizing the diversion.

They arrived at the ranch after Tom and Ann had left to go to town for the day. Mori and Mark checked the corrals, the buildings, and the house. Finding everything in order, Mark suggested they ride to Steamboat and Tugboat Rocks.

"Those are favorite spots of mine," Mark said. "It'll be a good workout for Sunny but not so much she should get too tired. I think she's itching to show me what she can do."

"I'm game. I remember seeing the rock formations when I use to ride my bike this way, but your uncle always chased me away before I could explore them."

Mark laughed. "I can believe that." He led the two horses into the corral and saddled them.

"Maybe we should take a lunch and some water," Mark said.

"I can fix it. Think Ann will mind if I rummage in her cupboards?"

"No. Go ahead. I'll lead the horses over to the house as soon as I'm sure Sunny can make the trip."

He watched Mori walk to the house, appreciating her determined stride and a crazy magic swooped through him. He'd never taken anyone but Rob with him to the formations that dominated the view from every corner of the ranch. He wanted to show Mori his "place" as he thought of it.

Mark made his way to the house to pick up Mori. He liked Sunny Day's stride. She moved easily, seemingly having little if any pain in her leg. Mori met him at the gate with thermos bottles and lunch sacks. Mark put them in the saddlebags.

"I used Ann's homemade sourdough bread for our sandwiches. Hope she won't mind."

"She won't. She's proud of her bread."

As they rode the two horses through the red rock cliffs and deep arroyos, Mark was well-aware of the heightening and intensifying feelings for Mori. Good or bad, his craving for her was strong. They were not mechanical reactions that had become a part of him for the past four years. He felt a mystique about the bond that seemed to tie him to her. It was like a spiritual experience.

They rode the two horses in comfortable silence for some distance, Mark glancing at Mori several times. Sometimes their eyes met and Mori smiled, sending waves of warmth through him. He wondered about her feelings and recalled the pleasure of the emotion he had felt when she touched her body against his. At a wire gate Mark dismounted to open it.

"The Overland Trail Register Cliff is up this draw some hundred feet," he said.

Mori glanced toward a burnt-orange, smooth sandstone cliff that was uplifted from the surrounding hills.

"We can walk to the cliff face." Mark put the bottom

end of the post in a wire circle and pulled a second wire over the top.

"I think I always got scared off your property by your uncle even before I got to this place," Mori laughed.

When they reached the cliff, Mori traced her right index finger over the carved letters of a stagecoach traveler who had passed the rock in 1859.

"Graffiti never seems to go out of style."

"No. There are pictographs on one side of Tugboat Rock. The Indians didn't miss leaving their signatures either."

The two poked around the hotel-sized cliff for several minutes before returning to their horses to continue their ride down Washboard Hill. At the bottom of the rocky track, they came to a few log poles and a stone foundation that were the remains of an old building.

"This was a saloon," Mark said. "Guess after a ride down Washboard in a swinging, swaying, dusty coach, travelers needed to fortify themselves for the next lap." Digging around in the saddlebags, Mark pulled out a thermos. "How about joining me for a drink of lemonade or coffee, whichever you made, before we move on?"

They sat on the short tough grasses, backs against the foundation, out of the sun and wind. Mark poured the drinks into folding cups and handed one to Mori. With her head back, Mori watched the white clouds that skimmed across the blue sky. Her serene face sent lightning charges through Mark.

"I camped out here when I was a kid. There's a spring

in the draw to the east of us. It was an adventure for me," Mark said.

"A perfect place. I'd have liked it," Mori said.

Mark reached out and brushed her brown hair from her cheek. Sitting next to her, Mark was afraid to breathe, afraid to break the spell that seemed to hold them as one. Not trusting his emotions, he stood as soon as they finished their lemonade and helped Mori to her feet. While he put away the cups and thermos, Mori mounted Midnight. Mark took a deep breath, hoping his shoulders would not betray his feelings.

They rode past rock rings that once anchored Indian tepees. "Digs by archaeological teams found that these rings were left by small groups of Indians as long ago as 3000 B.C. That is amazing to me. They even had pottery. The last Indians in here were probably the Comanche in the early part of the 1800s."

"But can you imagine a more picture-perfect place?" Mori looked across the broad plain dotted with colorful summer flowers and deepening shades of new grasses toward Tugboat and Steamboat, two towering wind-eroded shapes that protruded high above the surrounding hills and prairie.

Mark never wanted the morning to end. In his mind he contrasted Mori with Denise who had no wish to visit the ranch, thinking ranching a demeaning occupation. Mori seemed to enjoy the ride. He liked to watch her expressions of delight when they spotted an antelope with a new fawn, or the sharp-shined hawk that circled above them and then flew toward the juniper-covered hills, or the calves that kicked their heels and ran to their mothers when they rode through a small herd of cattle.

"I'm glad you're keeping the ranch. I'd hate to see all this turned into forty-acre tracts with houses on every knoll."

"I know. I think I'm a throwback to my great grand-father. I could easily live his life, outlaws, Indians, rustlers, all of it. Sounds stupid. Like a kid."

"No. I romanticize about history."

"Unfortunately, we can't go back. So I make my living as a lawyer, an acceptable profession for the Larsons, and support the ranch until I've paid off my mortgage. I want it to stay as it is."

"Do I hear a note of bitterness?"

"No. I'm happy I can manage, but someday I want to give up my practice and move to the ranch." Mark recalled how Denise would mock him and constantly urge him to sell the ranch. Mori appreciated his sentiments.

They came to the remains of a foundation near a second gate. A windmill creaked, rhythmically pumping water through a small pipe into a metal stock tank.

"Some forgotten homesteader staked out 160 acres here back in 1890s, but couldn't make it. That Homestead Act caused a lot of heartbreak in this country. My great-grandfather purchased the place and added it to the ranch."

Mori dismounted and poked around the rubble. "It looks like he built to stay. Stone walls, three rooms, and a well."

"Yes. Even considered the view and the wind, building here on the lee side of Steamboat Rock."

"Wonder what happened to him. Did he have a family?"

"Well, come with me." Mark took Mori by the hand and led her uphill into a stand of juniper to a small headstone.

"Oh," Mori caught her breath. She read, "Lucy Burns—Born September 22, 1889—Died April 15, 1893. How sad, just a baby."

"My uncle put up the headstone when the wooden marker collapsed," Mark said. "The family sold and left the area that summer."

They returned to the windmill and walked along the bottom of a draw to avoid the thick growth of squaw currant and mahogany that grew on the northeast slope as they headed for Steamboat Rock. The draw disappeared and they scrambled over loose slabs of red and orange sandstone toward sheer smoothly eroded cliffs. Bright splotches of lichens, mosses, and liverworts gave the appearance of a painter's pallet to the rocks. From a nearby shrub a Rufous-sided towhee broke the silence with a "Drink-you-tea, drink-your-tea" song.

About two-thirds of the way up the slope, they came to the steep-sided, jagged rock formation that circled at the base of Steamboat Rock. Mark picked his way over the loose slabs and gave Mori a hand. They came out on the saddle between Tugboat and Steamboat. A narrow grass-and-shrub-covered bench circled the next series of cliffs that led to the summit of Steamboat.

"Come on. There's only one way to the top that I know." Mark led Mori. "Watch your footing and for rattlers. They like to sun themselves on these ledges."

Mori shuddered. "Ugh!"

They followed the ledge that seemed to disappear near the pointed bow-like formation that gave the rock its name.

"Looks like were not going to find a way to the top. How did early pioneers ever get up there?" Mori asked.

Without comment, Mark led Mori to a deep crevice that ran from where they stood to the flat summit of the rock. Mori studied it, concerned that she could not stretch and reach from foothold to foothold, handhold to handhold. Exposure also disturbed her. "I think I'm destined to stay right here."

"We'll get there." Mark hoisted himself up the wall with the grace of a mountain lion to a narrow shelf and squeezed between the sheer walls. Then he reached a hand for Mori. "Take steps by pushing your feet into the rock spread-eagle fashion while I help you up."

For a moment Mori hesitated, not sure she should trust him. Then she did as told. Mark pulled her toward him. They stood face to face, body next to body, on the narrow ledge. His breath stirred her dark hair. With a devilish grin, Mark kissed Mori. He felt her body tremble.

"Like that?"

"No. I'm afraid I'm going to fall." The words came out in a hushed whisper.

"I'd never allow that." Knowing physical action would control his desire, he pressed against the sandstone and scrambled over a bulging outcrop to a series of steps that led to the summit.

He tossed his saddlebag to the top and straddled the bulge. Leaning forward he grabbed Mori by the hand and helped her up. The final climb was short and easy over loose slabs. The summit was wind-eroded, dotted with protruding rock pillars. Gusts of wind chewed away loose wafer-sized rock that sounded like coins thrown on a counter.

Mark watched Mori's expression when she looked out and over the rolling foothills that led to the deep river-cut canyon and the buildings of the ranch. The wind whipped her hair away from her face, giving her a soft vulnerable quality that disconcerted him.

Putting his arm around her waist, he said, "If you follow the course of the river north from our buildings you can see a steep cliff."

Mori nodded her head.

"That's an old buffalo jump. My grandfather decided to make the land above the cliff into a hayfield. When he started leveling the land, he uncovered ancient, fence-like lines of piled rock that led to the cliff so he contacted the university. They discovered artifacts and bones and dated the jump back hundreds of years. The hayfield was never completed. I'll take you to the jump sometime."

Mark turned toward Mori. He caught the tenderness in her eyes that made his heart pound so loudly he was certain Mori could hear it above the wind.

Picking up the saddlebags, Mark led Mori toward the stern of Steamboat Rock and to the sheltered side of the tallest pinnacle that was a vivid red against the brilliant blue sky. The sharp acrid scent of bitterbush wafted upward and was carried away by the strong west wind. Mark brushed the powderlike dirt from a flat rock. With a mocking, gracious bow he offered Mori a chair.

"This is the finest view, we have, ma'am. Hope you enjoy it." He sat on another slab of rock at a right angle from her and took out the lunch. "It appears that for lunch we have roast beef and cheese sandwiches, chips, carrots, oranges, and cookies—the last a specialty of the cook for the day."

"Sounds perfect. I did the best I could."

"Some coffee?"

Mori nodded her head. "Emily would love it up here."

"We'll bring her."

"We'd never get her up those rocks."

"I brought Rob here when he was six, on my shoulders, just before he was killed. I'm so glad I did."

The terrible pain in his eyes and the sadness of his look affected Mori deeply, but she resisted the urge to reach out to comfort him.

"I had to watch him. He was hyperactive, but that day he clung to me. He was an affectionate, loving little boy." Mark felt as though a heavy burden was being lifted from him as he spoke. His clenched fingers relaxed. "Denise was a heavy drinker. She loved parties and never believed that one or two cocktails could hurt our unborn child. Rob was born with fetal alcohol syndrome. We didn't know the cause of his problems at the time, but he had all the symptoms. Denise couldn't stand having a child who wasn't perfect and blamed my family for his problems. We put him in a special school because he couldn't keep up with other kids his age. It was so unfair to Rob to be cheated by Denise and her drinking."

His voice was barely audible. Mori sat quietly, straining to hear his words that fell from his lips. His body motions were tense and Mori yearned to touch him but knew it would stop him from speaking. It was as though he was alone on the rock, his grief plummeting over the cliffs to be picked up and conveyed by the wind into an unknown abyss.

He paused. As he talked about Rob, he felt the weariness and sadness he carried within disappear.

Mori waited for him to continue, but he did not. The passing of a cloud that covered the sun brought Mark out of his thoughts.

"Did you spend a lot of time on the ranch when you were young?" Mori asked to change the subject that was so painful to him.

"Not as much as I wanted. My mother always had a full agenda planned for my siblings and me—soccer, tennis, body building, dance lessons that I hated, time for summer camp—you name it. What about you?"

"I loved horses like many young girls. Once the Ridings told me I could help at the farm, I spent most of my time on the farm." She smiled. "Sometimes my mother insisted I do other activities which I did dutifully until I could go back to the farm."

"And when you came home after your divorce, you bought into the farm."

"It was a dream come true. At first I couldn't believe it, but it was true and I'm making a home for Emily."

He stood and gathered the remains of their lunches and put them in the saddlebags.

"I'll show you something before we leave."

Mori followed him along the flat ridge that narrowed near the bow. Looking straight ahead she managed to walk across it. Mark stopped below the last rock tower that rose above the summit. Engraved in the red-orange sandstone were the names of Charlie Larson, Mark Larson, Mark David Larson, Rob Larson.

"As long as I live I'll carry the memory of Rob's smile when I added his name."

Mark reached for Mori's hand and led her finger across the name of Rob. Her chest seemed to constrict, her breathing became shallow. She wanted to comfort the anguish she could sense within Mark but suspected he would resent her reading his feelings. She could not look into his face without revealing the desire she had for him. A feeling of intimacy filled the space between them.

They didn't speak, knowing any words would jar the magic of the moment. Only the wind that whistled around the cliffs and rattled the flakes of sandstone disrupted the silence.

Mark took Mori's chin in his hand and kissed her gently. She didn't protest or pull away as Mark put his arms around her and pressed against him. She responded by folding her body into his. They kissed more deeply as they embraced one another. Mark sagged against the cliff and slid to a sitting position, pulling Mori with him. She removed his arms from her waist and scooted to one side.

Far in the distance a herd of cattle grazed, looking no more than small bugs inching their way toward Steamboat Rock. A sharp piercing scream forced them to look above the rock. A golden eagle catching a warm draft of air appeared motionless as it rode the wind higher above them into the cobalt sky.

Mori felt estranged from her body and world below her. Though her exterior attitude appeared relaxed, she was not. She was very aware of Mark, his breathing, his movements, his nearness to her, his kiss that lingered within her and her reactions.

Mark picked up small chips of sandstone and tossed them over the edge of the cliff, never wanting the closeness he felt toward Mori to end. He controlled the magnitude of his yearning for Mori. It shattered his belief in himself and his determination to remain unattached to another human being afraid of what it might do to him. He had found a sense of accord within himself and his memories of his small son. Mori was breaking down the shell he had so carefully built around himself.

"If you didn't get to the ranch too often, why do you care about it now?" Mori asked.

"I did come here and spend as much time as I could. My parents sent the three of us if they were too busy with their activities to bother with us. That happened often enough. My sister and brother hated it and couldn't wait to get back to town. I never wanted to leave."

"What happened to them?"

"Cole manages the store. Beth is married to an orthopedic surgeon and lives in Texas."

Mark got up and pulled Mori to her feet. He held her close. "Day's passing. Got to feed the livestock so guess we'd better head for the ranch."

Mori moved away from him and walked to the small cut in the cliff and let herself down with small jerks and jumps where she could not reach with her feet, ignoring her fear of exposure. Mark admired her graceful movements as she picked her way down the cliff toward the mahogany-covered slopes below the cliffs.

They returned to their horses and rode side by side across the high rolling hills and over the arroyos that cut through the land. At the ranch, Mori helped Mark remove the saddles from the horses, curry them, and feed them grain. Mark checked Sunny Day's injury, carefully running his hand over her chest and toward the wound on her leg. Sunny stood like a rock.

"I don't think I've ever seen a horse recover the way she has," Mori said as she watched Mark and the gentle way he handled the mare.

"It's a mystery, all right," Mark mused. "She's done well today."

"It's called care," Mori said.

With horses left in the corral, the few cows and calves still in pasture near the buildings watered and fed, Mori and Mark walked toward the house, shoulders touching. She heard Mark catch his breath. He paused and taking her around the waist, swung her toward him.

"You're beautiful you know. More so than when I first helped you out all those years ago." He raised her chin. His lips brushed her cheek.

Mori laughed. "There you go again with your flattery, but thank you. I must tell you, I didn't like you much. You were so uppity."

"It's not flattery and I thought you were hotheaded," Mark replied with a chuckle.

"I like you much better now that I know you," Mori said.

"I certainly hope so, but I'll do anything you ask to improve your attitude."

Changing the subject, Mori said, "I really should return to the farm. I feel so guilty leaving Cecile with all the chores."

Why, she wondered, was she falling in love with the wrong man again? Running home was her only protection against the longing she had for him that stormed and thundered through her veins. She missed seeing the disappointment registered in his eyes.

"I'll take you, but you know Cecile can manage," he argued. "And until Tom and Ann get back, it's hard for me to leave."

"Yes, I know. I shouldn't have come." Her voice was cool, constrained, her manner displaying indifference in an attempt to cover her uneasiness. Mori ran up the stairs of the porch. Mark came two steps at a time and caught her hand of the door knob just as she opened it. For a moment he held her looking into her face trying to read her thoughts.

She steeled herself against his advances, determined she would not become another woman to be conquered and cast aside by him. A part of her blazed with love that she had carefully buried in her subconscious after the hurt she suffered from Frank. She forced herself to turn away and walk into the house. Her instinct for self-preservation warned her to flee. Mark sighed and followed her.

She paused. "Actually, I've really enjoyed the day, but I still feel guilty about leaving Cecile even if Jake is there to help."

Mark glanced at his watch. "Ann and Tom should be here shortly. I'll make us supper and coffee if you don't mind waiting that long."

Mori nodded her head in agreement. "I can give you a hand."

They had finished their meal of ground steak, fried potatoes, corn, and salad when Tom and Ann drove into the yard.

Pushing his chair aside, Mark went to the door to greet them while Mori rinsed and put dishes in the dishwasher.

"How was your day?" Ann asked as she came into the kitchen carrying two sacks of groceries.

"Wonderful. We enjoyed your bread and cookies for lunch."

"Good. Hope you're spending the night." Ann dropped the sacks on the counter.

"I've got to get home. We were just waiting for you."

Ignoring the protests from Tom and Ann, Mark and Mori left the ranch. They arrived long after dark at Riding Farm.

Chapter Thirteen

Two days after Mori visited the ranch with Mark, Frank arrived at the farm. Frank took off his jacket and tossed it into his car. He loosened his tie, ran a tissue across his forehead and dropped it to the ground. Except for the dog barking at him, the farm appeared deserted, although Mori's pickup stood in her driveway and two cars were parked in front of the office.

With long strides, Frank went to the door of Mori's house and rang the bell. While he waited for her to answer the door, he moved impatiently from one foot to the other. The dog kept his distance but continued to bark furiously, the bark echoing off the buildings. Annoyed, Frank picked up a pebble and threw it at the dog. Punch snarled. After waiting several minutes, Frank turned and headed for the barn, with the dog still nipping at his heels.

"Shut up!" he ordered.

Punch ignored him. Suddenly Witch dropped out of a cottonwood. She let out a "yarl," startling Frank.

"Damn animals. When I take over this place you're both out of here. Don't care if you do belong to Em."

As he walked along, Frank surveyed the farm with the attitude of ownership. The past year his sales record had been impressive. Now he wanted to invest. Mori had done well, he admitted. The farm and her horse business prospered. But more importantly, the land had tremendous developmental potential, and once he controlled Mori's interest and bought out Cecile's half ownership, Shawna had a buyer for the property who was willing to pay big bucks. He rationalized—his support payments for Emily were paying for the farm, so technically it was his. He admitted to himself that Mark was an interference to his plans and he needed to deal with him. One of life's set backs. Nothing serious.

It had been his good luck on one of his trips to the city near the farm to run into Shawna while he was in a coffeeshop having breakfast. They sat next to each other. It didn't take her long to convince Frank that he had to re-marry Mori to get control of the farm.

There was nothing Frank enjoyed more than a game. He believed completely in the saying "A sucker is born every minute," and his ability to bring anyone around to his way of thinking. Convincing Mori of his love for her and his regrets over his behavior would be simple enough once she realized the importance of having the family back together for Emily's sake. His objective was to marry her, sucker that she was. He held those with feelings of right and wrong as stupid. Fortunately, Mori had a conscience and that would help him marry her a second time for Emily's sake, he convinced himself.

While Frank listened to Shawna, he knew feelings of sentiment and love were signs of weakness. Even Emily, his own flesh and blood, garnered little affection, though he'd faked his fatherly love with her often enough. Listening to Shawna and the greed in her voice, Frank focused on the importance of getting Mori's property. He and Shawna had much in common and when it was all over, he knew they could have a relationship.

As Frank surveyed the property, he planned how he would ease the developer and Shawna out of any share in the profit of the farm once he married Mori. A sudden jerk of a smile appeared on Frank's mouth registering his cynicism. He brushed his sweaty palms along the sides of his pants and pulled out his cigarettes, pausing to light one before stepping into the office.

The room was deserted. The dog no longer barked at him but he could hear the *rr* of a tractor along with a rhythmic *clung kr clung* off in the distance.

Mori's old bag of a partner might create a problem, but he was certain that once he remarried Mori, he could talk Cecile into selling out. At her age she should be glad to leave.

Frank didn't doubt for a moment he could convince Mori to marry him. She had been crazy about him from the time they met, and he remembered how hurt she'd been over the divorce. That was to his advantage. Thank god the kid was in school. He could abide kids but not for long, not even Emily. He was glad he didn't have to take her for the summer.

At the corral, Frank leaned against the closed gate. He tossed his cigarette to one side and swatted a fly that landed on his neck. When he was in charge, he'd spray the bluebottles that buzzed around his head. He'd dispose of the horses and get rid of that unpleasant smell of horse sweat, manure, and urine too.

Looking past the corral toward the pond, his eyes narrowed in greedy anticipation as he calculated the dollars the farm would bring to his pocket. There was no question about the value of the farm. With the pond, the view of the mountains, the location not far from the state park, a developer could turn the 240-acre farm into expensive ten-acre plots. Certain that he could persuade Mori to get back with him, Shawna and he convinced a developer to spend the day checking on zoning laws. The developer wasted no time probing Frank's plan of action.

The noise of a vehicle entering the yard distracted Frank. When Frank saw Mark get out of his four-wheel drive, he cursed, but then decided that his dealing with Mark would be quick and to the point. He watched Mark come toward him.

Sunny Day nickered and trotted across the corral. She

approached the gate where Frank leaned, nudged Frank to one side, and slobbered on his shirt sleeve. Frank cursed and slapped at the horse. "Get away, damn you." Sunny whinnied a greeting to Mark, showering Frank with mucus.

"Well, look who's here, lawyer boy himself," Frank leered.

"Hello. What are you doing here?" Mark asked in an unfriendly voice.

Frank saw that his presence irritated Larson. It gave him a sense of satisfaction. "Holding down the fort till Mori gets back. Told her I would." Frank sucked on a second cigarette and exhaled smoke into Mark's face.

"Where is she?" Mark sounded surprised.

Frank thought quickly and then answered, "Out with the horses, where else?"

"Where are Cecile and Jake?"

"Don't know." Whoever Jake is, he said to himself.

"If you tell me which way Mori went, I'll see if I can give her a hand."

"Won't be necessary. Guess Mori didn't tell you. We're getting back together."

Mark's mouth opened in disbelief.

Frank took advantage of Mark's surprise and suspicion.

"Doing it partly for Em, but for us too. Mori never did like the idea of our divorce. Guess she's tried single living long enough. Anyway she called and asked me how I felt about it."

"Mori is a person who does stand by her commitments," Mark said.

Frank shrugged his shoulders but picked up the hurt in Mark's voice. He dropped his cigarette and ground it out, laughing to himself. It was almost too easy.

Mark petted Sunny under her chin and patted her neck. In a quiet voice he said, "Guess I'll take you out tomorrow." To Frank he said, "Well, congratulations. Hope things work out for the two of you. Tell Mori I'll call."

Frank didn't like the tone of disbelief in Mark's voice. "Won't be necessary. I'll relay your message."

"Thanks. But I'll call anyway."

"I'd rather you didn't."

"Oh."

"Well, you know, I have this thing about Mori," Frank said. "Don't like getting her upset."

"I'll need to talk to her about Sunny Day."

"Won't have to. I'm taking over some of the management." Frank almost laughed at Mark's expression as he made his way to his vehicle.

After Mark drove away, Frank wandered to Mori's house, anxious to get out of the heat and away from the bugs. He opened the door and let himself in. How trusting she is.

Everything is left unlocked. Someone could steal her blind. He went to her kitchen to find a drink, opening cupboard after cupboard as he hunted for some scotch or bourbon. Finding none, Frank looked in the refrigerator for a beer. Then he remembered Mori's aversion to alco-

hol, so he opened a soft drink and returned to the living
room where he sat down and propped his feet on the coffee table. He removed a cigarette and then scanned the
tables in the room for an ashtray. Not finding one, he
stood and returned to the kitchen where he took a porce-
lain saucer from the cupboard. Seated again, he drank
from the can of pop and inhaled his cigarette, blowing
smoke rings into the air for diversion. Mori, he saw, still
had her paintings hung on the walls. He'd always dis-
liked them and thought she was a lousy painter. Modern
art was more to his taste, and he was certain he could
manipulate Mori into replacing her art with his choices.

She's putty, he smirked.

He planned in his mind the ways he would keep the
money from the sale of the property to the developer.
And he would need to deal with Shawna. Ashes dropping on the carpet brought him out of his reverie. Mori
would be all over his case for being careless. If he
wanted her back, he would have to placate her, at least
part of the time. He rubbed the ashes into the carpet with
the toe of his shoe.

Frank glanced about the room. She had always been
too damn neat. She hadn't changed, still fussy by the look
of the house. He moaned as he thought about the times
she had nagged him to pick up his shoes, hang up his
clothes, and put his sales samples away until he'd lose
his temper and leave. It really was her fault, he rationalized, that he sought the company of other women.
She was noscy too, probably knew about his affairs

throughout their marriage, but she was so clingy. What a chump she was never wanting to admit the truth. He would have to tolerate her again but only long enough to gain control of the property.

Finished with his drink and cigarette, Frank found the bathroom and relieved himself. He flushed the toilet and wandered along the hall peering into Emily's bedroom, the guest bedroom, and Mori's room. Everything was in place, bed made, clothes put away. Mori's signature.

Frank left the house to look for her. He returned to the corral, opened the gate, went inside, and leaned against a watering tank. He pulled out another cigarette and lit it.

Before he caught sight of Mori, Frank heard her voice and those of some other riders. His impatience increased as he waited, cursing under his breath their slow progress to the barn.

As Mori and three women rode into the corral, their laughter all but drowned out the noise of the insects buzzing around his head. Frank studied the women with interest, wondering which one would be good for a date. At the moment, he was involved with the secretary in the main sales office in his hometown. She believed everything he told her. He also had a sales clerk who shared an interest in Chinese food with him, and there was a teacher living in one of the towns in his territory who did his bidding. He chuckled to himself at the gullibility of women. He would need a respite from Mori once they were married.

Remarrying her would pose problems with his outside

interests, but he decided he could find some reasonable excuse for frequent nights away from the house. It hadn't been difficult in the past. Frank caught the startled expression on Mori's face when she entered the corral and saw him. She dismounted with ease, said something to the three women, and then stomped toward Frank. It satisfied his ego to see the effect he thought he still had on her. Given time, he'd have her under his finger.

"Hi, beautiful."

"What are you doing here? We don't allow smoking in this area, or can't you read the sign over the barn door?" She emphasized the words.

"Ah, Mori, what you so grouchy about? Here I come with a peace offering and you're all over my case before I get a chance." Frank's voice carried a certain amount of anguish and his eyes conveyed pain and hurt at her words. He turned his head slightly so that the sun highlighted his blond hair and cast soft shadows on his face, illuminating his cheekbones.

"Put the cigarette out." Mori's nostrils flared in anger, revealing the distress he still caused her.

Frank ignored her as he inhaled. "Do you always have to be so cranky?"

Mori reached out and grabbed the cigarette from his fingers. To display her anger, she crushed it with the toe of her boot until the embers were dead.

"Say what you've got to say and get out of here." Mori clamped her teeth together and waited for an answer.

"I want us to talk as soon as you get rid of those three."

He studied the women with the eye of someone examining fine pieces of sculpture, deciding he would make a pass at the brunet who was the first one out of the barn. He caught her eye. The woman returned Frank's stare with a coquettish turn of her head. Disgust shot from Mori's face.

Mori called to the woman, "Would you lead the horse to the pasture and remove the bridle?"

"Sure," her voice carried a flirtatious tone to Frank. To her companions she called, "I've got to hurry." She led the horse to the pasture and came back to the barn. "See you next week, Mori." Hips swinging with sexual verve, she walked past Frank who whistled softly and opened the gate.

"Hello. I'm Frank Jordan, Mori's ex."

"I'm Lucy Hunter."

Mori walked toward the other two women to help them with the horses but did not miss the interchange between Frank and Lucy. Seduction, Mori decided, was still one of Frank's best talents as she watched him shuffle his feet, hang his head in a humble, self-effacing manner that usually ingratiated him with women who immediately wanted to mother him. The clouds moved away from the sun, casting a harsh light on his face, revealing lines of hard living, distracting some from his good looks. It pleased Mori to see him exposed.

Lucy thanked Frank for opening the gate and continued to her car. She'd freely given her name. That was a come on, he thought. He'd call her that evening and find out more about her. She might be the relief he would need from Mori once they were back together.

After helping the other two women deliver their horses to the pasture, Mori accompanied them to the gate where Frank stood waiting to open it.

The women paused, obviously expecting Mori to introduce them to Frank. When she didn't, Frank said, "I'm Frank Jordan, Mori's husband." They smiled, introduced themselves, and left the corral.

"See you next week," the women called to Mori.

As they walked away, Frank heard one comment to the other, "He's so good-looking. Why do you suppose Mori left him?" Frank smiled in gratification, pleased that the women were discussing him. It fed his ego to know he impressed most people, especially women. Mori groaned and Frank thought he had her where he wanted.

Mori waited for Frank to speak as he tried to read her thoughts. He couldn't, and that aggravated him. He prided himself on his ability to understand the emotions of other people and to determine how to use them. Mori had always been an open book but he admitted he was baffled by her attitude.

"What do you want, Frank?" Mori's words were cold and without feeling.

He had just impressed those women. How could Mori be so icy? Couldn't she see what an asset he could be to her? He just didn't get it. Most women were won over with a little sweet talking, but he guessed he was going to have to turn on the charm with Mori. She was so blind.

"Honey, I've come on a peace mission. No need to be ugly." He paused, wanting a response, but Mori simply stood waiting for him to continue. He felt uneasy, smarting under her cold attitude.

"I'd like to take you to dinner. I miss you and want us to consider getting back together. You know, I made a mistake. I love you and Em, and I'm tired of coming home to an empty house." He pleaded his case with his hands as well as his words, using his charm to appear helpless and lost.

Mori laughed out loud, insulting Frank.

How dare you insult me. I still have power and control of you.

The moment was interrupted as Jake drove the tractor and hay baler into the yard.

"How did it go?" she yelled at Jake.

"Okay. Most got the cutting all up."

"Good."

"Can't we go to your house and talk," Frank interrupted.

"No. We have nothing to talk about." Her voice was acid.

"Well, how about dinner? Spruce yourself up. Bet you haven't had fun for a long time." Convinced that no one could show her a good time except him, he continued his ploy. "Honey, you need a little romance, I can tell." Once they were in a romantic setting, he would manipulate her easily enough.

Mori raised an eyebrow. "No. I want you off this property."

"Come on, Mori. What's wrong with you? We've always loved each other."

Mori made no comment and that exasperated Frank. He reached to run his finger over her cheek, expecting to arouse some desire in her. She slapped his hand to one side.

Trying another tactic, Frank said, "Where's Em? I've really missed the two of you."

Mori scowled, expressing her doubt at his statement. "She isn't home. She's at camp." Mori lied, something that distressed her even if it was to Frank.

"Where?"

"Too far for you to go. Besides you had your chance this summer and you blew it. Emily was really hurt when I told her you didn't want her for her usual two-week visit."

"Why did you do that?"

"Because it was the truth and you wouldn't tell her."

Frank reached out and gripped Mori's arm.

Mori shook herself away from him and flashed in anger. "Don't touch me again."

Jake came over to Mori. "Need some help?"

"Would you please see Frank to his car?"

"Yes, ma'am." Jake indicated with a nod of his head that he would walk with Frank.

"I don't need any escort," Frank said, his voice flowing with control. "I'll call you later, Mori. I love you too much to give up easily. I've made a mistake and you know it. You need to think about how you felt about me. I'll give you some time." As Frank turned to walk to his car, he accidentally stepped in a fresh, green pile of horse manure that squished under his expensive shoes. For a moment his veneer of smoothness and magnanimity disappeared. He cast Mori an angry glance.

"You need to bring a little of your fussiness to the corral," he snapped, attempting to pierce Mori's coolness with his stare, but she started to laugh, mocking him for his mistake.

"Watch your step," she snickered.

Frank walked along the gravel driveway, dragging his foot in an attempt to clean off his shoe. Before getting into his red sports car, he tried to light a cigarette. When the lighter continued to sputter, he tossed it toward the barn in frustration. Mori's laughter resounded, intensifying his anger. He suspected he had lost the first round of the game. He had miscalculated Mori and her reaction, but it was only the beginning of a renewed courtship. Besides, he'd work on Mori's mother and his kid.

Mom, as he called his mother-in-law, thought of him in the same terms as American apple pie. He smirked maliciously. He knew she would be on his side in his courtship of Mori. Jenny never saw him in reality. As for Em, Mori and he divorced when she was three but Em wanted a dad. Em told him as much. He could use Em to bring Mori around. Mori's dad might be an obstacle. Frank had never been able to push Dave around and he never let Frank call him Dad. Frank suspected his father-in-law knew about his infidelities, but Frank wrote it off as envy.

Driving away from the farm, Frank smiled to himself knowing he would make a bundle of money off the sale of the farm. He'd call Shawna and the contractor and meet them for dinner. Then he would contact Lucy Hunter and suggest they have a drink at a local bar. If she was married, so much the better. He'd ask her husband. Knowing the husband would make it that much easier to establish a relationship with Lucy. Playing a husband for a sucker added to the fun of the game.

Frank felt his senses sharpen and his mind quicken. Once he determined how he could convince Mori of his sincere desire to get back together, he would have clear sailing. Living in Omaha was a problem. Frank decided to look for an apartment in town. That way he would be closer to Mori to speed up his plans.

He opened the vents of his car. The smell of horse manure was repugnant. He hit his fist against the dash, venting his frustration for stepping in the pile that elicited Mori's contemptuous laughter.

He would make her regret her actions.

Chapter Fourteen

Somehow Mori controlled the turmoil Frank caused her. *Still trying what he does best, seducing, but not me this time.* Mori wanted nothing to do with him, lost any feelings she had for him long ago and would prefer not to see him, but there was Emily to consider. Despite her dislike and distrust of Frank, she had to think about Emily, but that he could suggest they get back together filled her with disgust. She had to think there was some motive behind his line of talk.

Before their divorce, Mori began to recognize that Frank lacked human warmth and depth. She remembered looking into his eyes once and the chill she had felt. His eyes were clear and empty. After moving to the farm and restoring her self-esteem, she developed a better insight and understanding about him and saw him for what he was, a man with no conscience. He was an untrustworthy, superficial man. How she remained blind to Frank and his shortcomings amazed her.

Mori led Sunny Day into her stall, gave her grain and water, and then brought in a mare with a new colt. She checked Emily's colt, Traveler, and put him out to pasture.

"Don't mean no offense, Mori, but how you ever got mixed up with that man is a puzzle to me," Jake scratched his head with his index finger after watching Frank depart.

"It's a puzzle to me too. But I do have Emily, the one good thing out of my marriage."

"Yup, she's purty special. Be glad to have her home."

"I'm going to get her tonight. I'm having dinner with my folks before we come back. When Cecile returns, would you tell her we'll be late and not to worry?"

"Sure will."

"I'll be on my way if you can finish here. Mark should be out soon. Tell him where I am. I can't wait any longer."

"No problem. Will do. See you tomorrow."

When Mori entered her house, she was immediately aware of the irritating smell of cigarette smoke. A pale blue haze floated in the air and, for a moment, Mori was overwhelmed with a sense of fear that was quickly replaced by caution. She saw Frank drive away, knew his car was nowhere in sight on the farm, but she didn't put it past him to return and harass her in private. She locked her door before emptying the cigarette butts smoldering on a saucer from her only good set of dishes.

"Damn him," she cursed out loud. "He has no right coming into my house."

As she returned to the house, she rubbed the cigarette stain with a tissue to remove it, fuming with indignation. Mori put the saucer in the sink and retrieved the empty pop can from her coffee table. Seeing the ashes ground into her carpet filled her with feelings of indignation. She carried the can into the kitchen, rinsed it, and threw it into her recycling container. A distasteful loathing flowed through her veins.

"Pig," she swore.

Mori showered and changed clothes. Before leaving she rummaged through her catch-all drawer in the kitchen for the keys to her house. Mori closed and locked windows and locked her doors.

On the thirty-mile drive to her parents' home, Mori repeatedly questioned Frank's motives. She ran through the reasons she could think of. Aware that he had recently broken off his relationship with the woman who moved in with him after Mori left could be one reason. Mori knew Frank needed the admiration of a woman, someone to look after his needs. But that Frank wanted Mori back was a question she could not answer. Whatever his reasons, she knew he would use her mother and Emily to achieve his goal. Mori intended to beat him at his own game.

As Mori pulled into the drive to park her truck, Emily burst out of the door to greet her.

"Guess what, Mama, Grandma took me shopping and bought me new clothes for school and we got all my supplies. They're neat and she got me a case to keep everything in place. I can't wait for school to start."

Mori hugged Emily. "You'll have to show me."

"The stuff is on the floor in the living room. I'm showing it to Grandpa. Come on." Emily tugged on Mori's arm.

"That you, Mori? I'm in the kitchen."

"Hi, Mom. Emily wants to show me her school supplies. I'll come in and help you in a minute. Hi, Dad."

"Hi, sweetie. Good to see you." Dave hugged his daughter.

"Look, Mama. See I've got new colors and paints and a whole box of pencils and a tablet and my workbooks." Emily picked up each item to show Mori.

"This granddaughter of mine is all set to outshine her classmates," Dave laughed.

"I've got new pants and shirt, and Grandma bought me socks to match. I'll try them on." Emily ran toward the bedroom. "I'll be right back."

Dave studied his daughter, waiting for her to speak. When she said nothing he commented, "You seem upset, Mori. Care to tell me about it?"

"Frank came to the farm this afternoon."

"What did he want?"

"Says he'd like us to get together again."

"Well, Mori?" her father paused.

"I'm not about to get mixed up with him again."

"Good. Never did trust him. Can't understand what your mother sees in him."

"I don't want to say anything that Emily might over-hear."

"Sure."

"See, Mama, my favorite colors." As Emily entered the room she twirled around in her deep pink, green, and blue outfit.

"Beautiful," Mori said. "It fits perfectly."

"I can wear it first day of school."

"It looks nice. Now I'm going to help Grandma."

"I can help too."

"Grandpa will get lonesome. I know he wants you to keep him company." Mori winked at her father.

"You bet. Let's play a game."

"Okay. Uno. I can beat you."

"See you both in a little while," Mori said.

As Mori entered the kitchen the smells of roast beef and freshly baked bread brought back memories of love and security. Mori hugged her attractive mother with affection.

"You arrived just in time. Dinner's about ready to put on the table. You can mash the potatoes."

"Frank came to see me this afternoon."

"Wonderful. Oh, I do hope you, Frank, and Emily become a family again." Jenny gave her daughter a kiss on her cheek.

"We won't, Mother, and I'd really appreciate it if you don't encourage him and don't try to manipulate Emily."

"Oh, Mori," Jenny stopped stirring the gravy. "I only want what's best for your happiness."

"Frank is the worst thing for me. I've never told you much about us because I know you loved Frank like a son."

"But he isn't and you are my daughter. Frank is such a nice man though." She paused. "I'm mom to him. He's the son your dad and I never had."

"Frank asked me to leave. He had another woman. He had several relationships with other women, but the last one, he insisted, was the love of his life. I just couldn't believe it, at first, though subconsciously I suspected it."

"Mori, you never told me." Jenny held the pan of vegetables over a bowl. Her expression registered her distress.

"It was hard for me to accept. I thought I had failed Frank. Now I know differently." The words were difficult for Mori to utter.

Jenny's eyes widened in disbelief. She rubbed her hands together nervously. "Mori, you should have told me."

"I was afraid you wouldn't believe me and, at the time, I was feeling so guilty, so lost, like I was facing death," Mori said. "I was so lonely so many nights. I use to lie in bed worrying that he had wrecked his car, or he was drunk and in jail, or mugged and maimed. Every time I heard a car I jumped out of bed to see if it was Frank. Not once did I suspect he was unfaithful."

Tears ran down Jenny's cheeks. She put an arm around Mori's waist. "I'm so sorry. I always thought we communicated well with one another. How could I have been so blind?"

"Frank has a way of deceiving people. I truly believed Emily would make a difference and Frank would stay home, but he always insisted his business had to come first. He wanted the best for us." Mori paused, her hands pressed on the cupboard as though giving her strength. "Anyway, if he calls you and I'm sure he will, please don't encourage him. I can't endure any more of him," Mori paused, swallowing her anguish and her pride, and then added, "and I have my health to think about."

"I promise, I won't talk to him again," Jenny said emphatically.

"Something else, Mom," Mori gulped almost afraid to say her thoughts, "I think I'm in love again." She put up her hand to stop her mother from making a comment. "I can't believe that this is happening to me. I know, I'm almost afraid to have romantic feelings, I should be practical, I have Emily, but I think I love Mark Larson." The words were out leaving Mori with a feeling of relief.

"First, we shouldn't be afraid of love. Secondly, and most important, does he love you?"

"I don't know but I think so."

"Be careful, dear. He hasn't the best reputation when it comes to women, especially since the death of his family. I don't want to see you hurt again."

"I know. I'm not going to push anything. I can only wait and see what happens."

During dinner Emily chattered about school, but Mori and her parents discussed nothing about Frank. They played games after dinner until late.

It was nearly eleven when Mori and Emily started home. In spite of the time, Emily talked and laughed most of the way to the farm. She reminded Mori of the small, noisy, Western kingbirds that resided in the cottonwoods at the farm.

Pulling into the driveway, Mori cut the engine. She noticed Cecile's car parked in front of her house and wondered when she had gotten home from the horse show in Estes Park. Reaching across Emily, Mori opened the truck door.

"We can unload your packages tomorrow," she said.

"Mama, I have to take them in now," Emily protested.

"Okay. You carry some, and I'll help. Now scoot. It's late and we've got to get to bed."

As Mori climbed out of the truck, she thought she caught the smell of smoke. She sniffed the air, sniffed again, and decided she was becoming paranoid. Digging into her handbag, she found the keys, and followed Emily to the door.

"Do you smell anything," Mori asked as she unlocked the door.

"Nope. Like what?"

"Never mind. I think my nostrils are playing tricks on me. I thought I smelled smoke."

Emily sniffed the air before entering the house. "Yuck. Smells awful in here. Yeah, I smell something."

"It's stale cigarette smoke. Go to your bedroom and get into your pajamas."

"Who'd you allow to smoke in our house?"

"No one."

Emily looked at her mother with a perplexed expression. "Was Dad here?"

"I don't think so." Mori crossed her fingers.

"I'm thirsty."

"Want some milk or juice?"

"Juice."

Mori deposited Emily's packages on a chair, dropped her purse next to the desk in the kitchen, poured orange juice, and took out crackers. She opened windows to air out the house.

"No more stalling," she told Emily when she finished her snack. "Get into your bed and I'll tuck you in."

Before undressing for bed, Mori walked around the house, inhaling deeply in an attempt to locate the source of the smoke she thought she smelled, then jogged toward the barn, checking the office and Cecile's house on the way. Nothing seemed out of the ordinary, although she caught a fleeting waft of something like smoke several times. If there was smoke she decided it was being carried from somewhere far off by the light night breeze or possibly she was imagining the smell because of her sensitivity to cigarette smoke. Mori returned to her house. She checked Emily and went to bed, falling asleep instantly.

Something kept triggering Mori's mind, willing her to wake up. She rolled over to look at the time, hoping it wasn't morning. The clock displayed 1:15 in red numbers. The drapery cord banged rhythmically against the window, weird shapes of light danced across the wall and there was that smell of smoke. Mori attempted to put it out of her mind as part of a bad dream but failed.

"Oh my! Oh no!" Mori bolted out of bed, staggered to the window and looked out. Orange flames licked up the east side of the barn and sparks shot through the sky like Fourth of July fireworks.

Grabbing her clothes, Mori dressed, buttoning her shirt as she ran toward the door. She paused long enough to see that Emily still slept. No time to wake her, Mori decided. At the door she pulled on one boot over her bare foot and hobbled outside still putting on the second one.

As she ran toward the barn, she heard the crackling and snapping of burning wood and felt the heat. Out of the corner of her eye she caught sight of Cecile coming from her house.

"I've got to get the horses out of the barn," Mori yelled above the noise of the fire. "Call 911."

"I have. Don't go in. Forget the horses. They can't be saved. You might be killed." Cecile chased after Mori to try and stop her.

Mori climbed the fence and raced to the barn doors. She yanked them open. A blast of heat hit her and she shielded her face with her arm as she entered the building to the screams of terror from the horses.

Flames ate up the far end of the barn. Mori grabbed a lead rope and threw open the gate to Sunny Day's stall. The mare reared, her eyes wild and glassy with fright. She attempted to rush Mori, but Mori caught her and snapped the lead rope to her halter. In the stall next to Sunny Day a young mother kicked at the sides of the wall as she whinnied her panic. A few feet away a support timber crashed to the floor. Mori led Sunny out of the stall fighting her the entire distance. In her terror the horse pulled against the lead rope in her attempt to turn and run into the flames. Sunny spun her buttocks left knocking Mori to one side, but Mori held onto the rope. Hay caught fire and raced toward the open stall door. Filled with terror, the mare bolted forward hitting Mori in the back with her nose and Mori lurched forward and fell. The horse dragged her over the floor as Mori fought to regain her footing. Perspiration ran down Mori's forehead into her eyes and smoke seared her lungs and stung her eyes. As Sunny Day lunged toward the back of the barn toward the roaring fire, Mori almost lost her footing a second time but again held onto the halter rope as she tugged and dragged Sunny toward the open barn doors. Near the entrance, Cecil grabbed the lead from Mori and took control of Sunny.

"Don't go back in there," Cecile screamed. Before Cecile could stop her, Mori ran back into the barn never hearing Cecile cry out, "Mori, Mori, you'll be killed."

Flames chewed along the stalls, crawling along the top of the divider that held the mare and her colt. The mare thrashed violently against the divider. Grabbing the second lead rope, Mori pulled open the gate to clip the rope to the halter. The mare lashed out with her left hoof, hitting Mori in the thigh. For a moment Mori swayed from the pain, bracing herself against a support timber that felt hot. Writhing from the blow, she struggled to snap the lead to the halter and slap the mare on her flank with the end of the rope. The mare bound forward, nearly picking Mori off her feet. The colt tried to come between Mori and the halter rope but Mori pushed him aside. He screamed and bit Mori and kicked at her with his hind legs. The mare bolted for the open gate while Mori worked the rope short to keep the horse from rearing. The colt whinnied and circled his mother. Heat scorched Mori's skin as the red-hot flames shot up the walls of the barn. She fought to keep the mare from running into the blazing inferno at the end of the barn with strength she didn't know she possessed. The mare reared pulling Mori off her feet. She held the rope and urged the colt toward the open doors.

The back wall of the barn crashed inward, sending flames racing toward Mori. The sleeve of her shirt caught fire. She held it against her waist to smother it as she labored to lead the horse outside. Now flames ate the wood on both sides of the alley. She smelled scorched hair. The wind fed the fire spreading it though the floor over her head. Mori dragged and pulled the horse into the open just as the entire second story floor collapsed. Once outside the mare braced her legs and refused to move. Heat scorched Mori's skin as she labored to pull the horse away from the fire. The mare trembled violently arching her neck. Her ears twitched nervously as she sought out her colt who paced behind the mare, nudging both Mori and his mother. Cecile had the gate to the pasture open.

"Get her over here while I keep the other horses at bay," Cecile called. "The whole bunch is headed this way."

Mori smacked the hindquarters of the mare forcing her to run toward the opening. The mare paused to stare at Mori and Cecile. Cecile picked up a switch and drove mother and colt into the pasture. In the pasture the horse sniffed her colt with her nose softly nudging him to her side away from the inferno.

Cecile closed the gate and put an arm around Mori. Tears streamed down her chalk-colored face. Together they moved away from the conflagration. Knowing the local volunteer fire department was too late to save the building, she paused at the gate to watch the force of the flames pierce through the roof.

Three fire trucks and an ambulance approached the corral, blue lights flashing, but Mori could not hear the sirens above the roar of the sheets of orange that moved in erratic patterns into the black of night.

Mori rubbed her arm over her soot-covered forehead to wipe away the perspiration that ran into her eyes. Neither Cecile nor Mori moved even though they were close enough to feel the searing heat of the fire against their bodies. Cecile reached out and took Mori's hand.

"You could have been killed. I don't know what I'd do if something happened to you. The horses weren't worth your life." She wiped her eyes with the sleeve of her shirt and forced down the sobs that were close to overtaking her.

Mori looked at Cecile. "I couldn't let Sunny Day die after what she's been through and the fight she put up and I would never get over letting the mare and colt die. I couldn't stand that."

Cecile shook her head and with her arm around Mori's waist, hugged her. "At least Emily and I still have you."

A fireman ran up to them and pulled them away from the collapsing building. "Anyone in there!" he shouted.

"No."

"Come on. Get away from here." He saw the burned sleeve of Mori's blouse. "You all right? Looks like you're going to have some blisters. Got your hair singed too. I'll take a look at your arm in the van over there." He pointed to the ambulance. The red lights swirling above the cab added to the hideousness of the night in Mori's mind. He led her to the vehicle. Cecile followed.

Firemen pumped water on the building but it did little more than sizzle and steam, intensifying the grotesque scene. Walls collapsed inward. As they crashed to the ground, sparks flew into the night sky. A high wind carried the embers into the pasture toward the newly cut alfalfa.

"We have hay down," Mori shrieked. "Those sparks will ignite it."

Leaving Mori and Cecile next to the ambulance, the fireman ran to one of the trucks. Mori and Cecile watched as he waved his arms and they saw a pump truck head through the corral and across the pasture to the hayfield. Mori dashed for the gate to close it before the horses saw it was open. Several corral posts smoldered and Mori shouted at the fireman to come with water to put them out before they burned too. The last support beams fell to the ground, pouring flames across the corral that nipped at Mori's heels. Some dry grass began to flame upward and Mori stomped, feeling the heat through the soles of her boots.

One of the fire fighters sent a stream of water across the posts while another led Mori to the ambulance to look at her arm. When Mori reached the van, she leaned against the side, feeling weary beyond comprehension. Her legs ached, her burns stung, and she shivered uncontrollably. A small figure approached Mori and Cecile.

"Mama, you didn't wake me and I was scared."

Mori stooped and held Emily close to her.

"You were sound to sleep. I didn't have time to wake you and I hoped I'd be back before you woke up."

"Are you hurt, Mama?" Emily asked.

"No. I have a few bumps and bruises."

"Why is the barn all burned up?" Emily started to cry.

"I don't know. Now wipe your tears. Everything is okay."

"Where's Traveler?"

"He's in the pasture. Stand between Cecile and me, and we'll keep you warm."

Cecile made room for Emily. The fireman approached them. "I'll look at your arm. You mind getting into the ambulance?"

"It's okay."

"Mori, let him look at it," Cecile insisted.

"Mama, you didn't tell me you were burned!" Emily cried.

"It's nothing. Don't cry." Mori pulled a tissue from Emily's pocket.

"Then let the man see your arm."

Inside the ambulance, the attendant studied Mori's arm. "Looks like a second-degree burn." He cut away the sleeve of the shirt and carefully washed the burned area with a sterile gauze pad, and soap and water, and wrapped her arm in a dry sterile dressing. For the first time, Mori looked at the burns. She shivered, feeling the early morning cold, and the fireman put a blanket over her shoulders.

"You better let us take you into the hospital and check out that arm. Hate to see you develop an infection."

Mori shook her head and crawled out of the ambulance. Tears filled her eyes and she dried them with her knuckles before Emily and Cecile could see them. Cecile led the way to a railroad tie where they sat and huddled together. The fireman brought a second blanket that he put over Cecile and Emily.

As the dark of night gave way to the light gray of dawn, nothing remained of the barn but a smoldering heap of black debris and sizzling orange embers. One of the volunteer fire fighters approached the three.

"We'll leave a couple of men to watch the area until the fire's completely out. Just hope the wind doesn't come up again. Hate to see it spread." He paused. "Got any idea what started this?"

Mori and Cecile shook their heads.

"Well, I'll report it, of course, and we'll do an investigation into the cause."

"We want to know. If we can be of any help please tell us," Cecile said.

"Sorry this had to happen. My two kids like coming out here to ride. They'll want to know if the horses are okay."

Mori attempted a smile. "They are. You can tell them we're open for business as usual." Mori slurred the words subduing her actual feeling of defeat.

The fireman nodded sympathetically. "Terrible loss, but we'll be out. My kids and I can maybe give you a hand in the clean up."

"Thank you," Mori and Cecile said.

Two trucks and the ambulance left. A man turned off the lights of the truck that remained and joined a second man. The two walked around the smoldering pile of cinders using an Indian pump to douse the hot spots. The air smelled strongly of soot and charred wood.

"I guess we ought to offer them some coffee and breakfast," Cecile said.

"Yes, I guess so." The impact of the loss had not yet registered in Mori's mind, but the sight filled her with depression. She felt too numb to stand.

Neither woman moved. They continued to sit too exhausted and distressed to make the effort. Emily leaned against Mori and took her hand. "Mama, everything will be okay, won't it?"

Chapter Fifteen

Mark climbed out of bed, opened his drapes, and stared at soft rain that was beginning to wet the sidewalks. The early light turned the morning into shades of gray. He dressed and went to his kitchen to make coffee, turning on his radio before walking to the door to retrieve his newspaper. Pausing at the door he inhaled deeply, enjoying the fresh smell of early morning and listening to the soft sounds of rain hitting the sidewalk.

During the night he promised himself he would seek out Mori and ask her about Frank rather than take his word. If what Frank had told him was true, Mark resolved to do everything in his power to dissuade Mori from remarrying him. She had taken hold of him, haunting his thoughts day and night and he knew he could not let her go without a fight.

Mark had tossed and turned most of the night arguing for and against the emotions and the love he admitted he had for Mori. Frank's announcement shocked Mark into recognizing his feelings for Mori and that if he didn't take action he might lose her.

For years, Mark did nothing to stop the rumors spread by Shawna that he was on the make for any good-looking woman, but could not commit himself to Shawna or anyone else until he resolved his grief over the loss of his family. Shawna's rumors became a shield to hide his fears of a repeat of his disastrous relationship with Denise and the death of his son. He didn't want to hide behind a shield any longer.

Shawna was aware of Denise's unfaithfulness and her drinking. At the time Mark hated to admit Denise was an alcoholic. After Denise's death he blamed himself for some of her problems and conceded that he made no effort to help her. For years he thought he could have prevented the death of Denise and Rob.

Mark sat at the table, filled his cereal bowl, and poured coffee. He opened his paper only half listening to the local news on the radio. The name Riding Farm jolted his mind and he laid the paper down. He caught the words "destructive fire levels barn," but the newscaster proceeded to another item. Mark switched to a different station. The weatherman forecast a rainy day. Mark pulled the plug on his coffeemaker and raced upstairs for his keys and jacket, frustrated that he had missed details about Riding Farm. He prayed the fire was at another location. Fear churned in his mind as he backed his four-wheel drive out of the garage. Anxiously, he ran his hand over his face and through his hair, afraid to turn on his radio again.

Stepping on the accelerator he drove out of town, hoping he would not be stopped for speeding. Although it was early, Mark called his secretary on his cellular phone knowing he might need to cancel his appointments for the day.

"Sorry to call you, but you have to cancel my morning appointments."

"What's wrong?"

"I'm not certain but I think there has been a fire at Riding Farm."

"Oh, I heard something about that on the radio. That's where you keep one of your horses."

"Yes."

"You are due in court at one this afternoon. Will you be there?"

"I'll try. If I can't make it, I'll ask Wilson to go in my place. I'll call."

"Hope your horse is all right."

"I hope Mori's all right," Mark answered. He replaced the phone in its holder and raced along the highway.

As Mark drove into the farm he smelled charred wood and the heavy odor of stale smoke. Pulling to a stop in front of the office, he saw immediately that the barn was gone. As he hurried toward the area of the destroyed building he searched for Mori and, at the same time, noticed the damage. Nothing was left of the tackroom and the barn except a smoldering heap of blackened cinders, some still glowing orange. He found Mori sitting with Cecile and Emily. They huddled together in the gray dawn, the cold drizzle wetting the blankets that covered them. As he passed the fire truck, he cleared his throat to announce his presence. Cecile and Emily turned to look at him. Emily half-smiled but Mori sat motionless.

"I'm so sorry about the fire." Mark put a hand on Cecile's shoulder. Where's—," he started to ask about Frank but stopped himself when he saw the two volunteer firemen but no one else. Squatting in front of the three, Mark studied their faces and read the anguish in their expressions.

"I heard about the fire on the news," he said. "I got here as soon as I could."

"Thanks for coming," Cecile said. "I'm afraid there's nothing you can do. Fortunately, Mori got Sunny Day out of the building before the walls started collapsing."

The sadness in Cecile's voice touched Mark's heart.

"The barn . . . Ben and I worked so hard to build it, and it's gone. I feel I've lost a part of my past," Cecile continued.

Mark reached out and touched Cecile's face. "We'll have to build a new one. You three have got to get out of this drizzle. The blankets are getting wet."

Mark lifted Mori to her feet and was struck by how

light she felt. He was filled with his love for her as he held her against him in the hope that he could comfort her, but Mori remained rigid and tense as a lion about to leap on prey. Reluctantly, Mark released his hold, determined he would help her reconstruct the barn. Mark gave Cecile a hand and then picked up Emily. Mori seemed in a trance, adding to Mark's deep concern. He wanted her to react to the disastrous fire or at least acknowledge his presence but she did not.

"Mori, we'll go to your house if it's okay. I know where things are and I'll fix breakfast while you three change clothes," Mark said. "And your arm. I've got to get you to the doctor."

Mori nodded her head.

"I can manage at home," Cecile said. "Emily can come with me while you take her to town."

"No," Mori's voice cracked. "You come with us. I don't need a doctor."

Hearing her voice flooded Mark with feelings of love as well as concern. After herding the trio into the house, he directed them to wash and change clothes. Mechanically Mori obeyed, but Cecile offered to help him.

"No, Take care of yourself and maybe try to shake Mori out of her lethargy."

"I'll try."

Mark retrieved clothing for Cecile from an office. By the time Mori and Cecile entered the kitchen Emily was already there helping Mark. When Emily saw her mother, she faced the door, a guilty expression on her face. Mori saw the dog and cat curled up on the rug in front of it.

"Mark thought it would be okay to bring Punch and Witch in the house this once. They were all wet too and don't have any place to go without the barn." Her small voice added a positive sound to the kitchen.

"It's fine," Mori answered. She walked toward the animals and gave each one a pat.

Mark pulled out chairs for Cecile and Mori and noticed Mori's arm.

"I'd better get you to the doctor as soon as we eat. That looks terrible."

"No. It isn't necessary. I just have a few surface burns." Her voice sounded apathetic and hopeless.

"It looks worse than that."

"I'm not going. I have too much to do." Her voice was heavy with weariness but a bit of her usual determination penetrated her words.

Mark scowled as he filled their plates with eggs, bacon, and toast and served coffee to Cecile and Mori. Emily ate everything Mark gave her but Cecile and Mori needed prodding.

"Hey, I'm going to be insulted if you don't eat the breakfast I made." Mark looked at Emily. "Anything wrong with it?"

"No way. It's good," Emily answered.

"Well, then, Mori and Cecile, start eating."

Cecile smiled and took a bite of egg, but Mori sat with hands folded in her lap, ignoring the food.

"If I acted like you, Mama, you'd get after me," Emily scolded.

"You're right, I'll try." Mori picked up her fork, then put it down and picked it up with her left hand. "The burns feel tight," she explained to the others.

Mark filled mugs with coffee and sat across the table from Mori. When he saw how tired she looked his pulse quickened. All he wanted to do was pick her up and try to comfort her, but he knew it wasn't the time.

"I'll give you an award for this breakfast," Emily chirped.

Mark smiled. "Thanks. How did the fire start?"

"We don't know," Cecile said.

"The fire inspector is sending out someone to check for possible arson but I can't imagine why anyone would want to destroy our barn." Mori's voice was controlled but puzzled.

A picture of Frank came into Mark's mind but he quickly dismissed the thought that he would start the fire. He had no reason to suspect Frank, if what he said were true . . . that he loved Mori and Emily.

"Whatever the cause, it couldn't have come at a worse time. School starts in three weeks and the college students will be back and there are Arabian horse shows around the state. We won't be ready for them and our tack is gone so we won't be able to offer rides or lessons and with no barn we can't take in boarders." Mori's thoughts and words tumbled forth revealing the distress she felt. She became quiet as a worried frown creased her forehead. Pushing away from the table, Mori expressed her concern with her hands. Mark had to control his desire to shelter her in any way he could but was certain she would resent it. He cursed her independence though it was one of the traits he admired.

"I just know I'll never manage my payments to you without an income," she said to Cecile.

"We have insurance." Cecile put her hand on Mori's good arm. "And I can wait for the payments. I don't want you to worry. We have too much to do to get back in business."

"The insurance will never cover everything we lost."

"We've still got the horses."

"But no tack. How can we rent horses without saddles? And we can't be ready fast enough."

Emily went to Mori and hugged her. "Mama, we'll work things out. Mark will help, won't you?"

Mark interrupted the women. "I'll help. I've got extra tack at the ranch." He paused. "True, all my saddles are Western but they'll work and I don't think most of your customers will mind. Some may bring their own."

"We haven't got room to put them with our tackroom gone," Mori protested.

Mark held up his hand. "Let me finish. You can turn the office into a tackroom for the time it takes to build a new one, and I've got a friend in the construction business. I'll get him out here to clean up the rubble from the fire so we can get bids on a new barn."

"We can't let you do that," Cecile said.

"Why not? You forget what friends are for. Now, who's your insurance agent?"

Cecile gave him the name of their company and representative.

"You three need to get some sleep. I'll make phone calls." Mark refused to accept their protests as he pushed them toward the bedrooms.

Once Mori, Cecile, and Emily were settled in bed Mark went to the corral to check the damage and the amount of rubble left by the fire. The rain, he was pleased to see, was helping to put out the last smoldering embers, although it created an unpleasant smell of scorched and charred wood. He walked toward the volunteer firemen who continued to circle the remains of the barn with hand pumps. Jake walked with them.

"Morning," Jake greeted Mark. "Sure had a holocaust here. Can't fathom how this happened? Everything was fine when I left last night. I checked and didn't spot nothing unusual." His voice quivered as if he blamed himself.

The volunteer fireman shook hands with Mark. "I'm Chuck. I've picked up on a theory about this fire but you got to realize I'm no expert and I probably shouldn't say anything."

"What's your theory?"

"Well, come around here with us. I was just about to show Jake." Mark walked with the two men and a second volunteer joined them.

"If you look here—see—this pile of manure seems to

have smoldered for some time. Kinda like a punk might do. It's bad stuff when it gets started. Then we had that wind during the night and I think it caused the grass to catch fire, blaze up, and move toward the barn. It's been dry the last several weeks so the weeds were ripe for fire." He paused, waiting for either acknowledgment or disagreement from the others. When they made no comment, he continued, "I suspect, someone tossed a cigarette or something and that's what started the whole thing. If we hadn't had the wind, it probably would have died right here, but you know how long it takes for a cigarette to burn itself out." He rubbed the stubble on his chin between his thumb and index finger. "We're lucky the wind blew in this rain. It isn't apt to flare up. Don't think we'll have to stay here much longer."

The volunteer's words stung Mark, filling him with anger and disgust. "Mori and Cecile don't allow smoking around the buildings," he said. A picture of Frank came to his mind. He had seen him smoking.

"Well, whether they do or not, this sure appears to have started from a cigarette. If it hadn't landed in that manure, it probably would have gone out," the fireman said.

Mark helped the firemen douse the smoldering embers and, by noon, the last were out. The volunteers left and Mark made calls to the insurance company, his ranch, and his friend. After checking Mori, Cecile, and Emily, Mark raced to town to meet his court session with his client. Jake agreed to watch for any flare-ups and to fix gaps in the fence until Mark returned to the farm, but the telephone rang continuously as neighbors and customers called to express their concern and to offer assistance.

The sound of a machine hovered in the background. It thrummed rhythmically, sometimes soft other times loud, pricking Mori's mind into consciousness. She opened her eyes. It was dusk. Rain pattered softly outside her open window cleaning the air of the burned wood smell.

Her first thoughts were of the hay. She relaxed when she remembered Jake baled it the previous day. They wouldn't lose their cutting, which was a relief. A black cloud crowded out the thoughts of the hay as she recalled the fire. She pulled the covers around her and shut her eyes trying to blank out the scene from hell. A feeling of hopelessness filled her lungs and she shuddered. She rolled over on her back catching her arm under her and gasped from the pain. Tears formed in her eyes and she reached for a tissue. The cool air tickled her good arm and she quickly put it under the covers. A sound of easy gentle breathing alerted her.

"Emily, are you here?"

"It's me, Mark. Emily went with Cecile to her house so you could sleep. Do you feel rested?" His voice carried concern. "Your burn must hurt awful."

"It does but it will heal. I'll get up."

"No need. You've got a real bruise on your leg."

"How do you know I've got a bruise?"

"Emily told me. She's worried about you." Mark hesitated before adding, "I am too."

Mark felt a hot cord of anger inside him at the effect the fire had on Mori. He wanted to lash out at the one who caused the destruction and vent his rage with his fists.

"It must be late. I'm ready to get up."

"Good."

"If you'll leave, I'll get dressed."

"I'll be in the living room. I've got lots of news to tell you." Mark switched on the light as he left. The sight of Mori sent bolts of lightning through him, sealing the love he felt for her forever. He wanted to help her out of bed, hold her, and declare his love. For now, he knew he had to retreat and control his desires. Mori needed time to collect her thoughts about the fire.

It surprised Mark how quickly Mori dressed and came into the living room. He remembered the hours it took Denise to dress. "That didn't take long."

"I'm a quick draw artist. You get that way on a farm." He heard her faint chuckle and it sent pleasant chills through him and a sense of relief. "I want to hear the news you have."

"Some is good, some not so good. Where do you want me to start?"

"The good."

"I like to hear that." Mark sat on the sofa and pointed to the seat next to him. Mori joined him. He handed her a cup of tea. For a moment Mark and Mori sipped the drinks in silence. Mark sorted through his mind for where to begin and what to tell Mori.

"I heard at the courthouse that a developer was looking into the zoning laws for your land."

Mori's mouth dropped open in surprise. "What?"

"You aren't selling the farm?"

"Oh, Mark, of course not." Mark could feel the anger rising in Mori and he heard her grind her teeth. For some reason it made him smile and he chuckled softly. Her independence and resolve was surfacing and Mark felt relieved.

"It isn't funny," Mori snapped.

"No." Mark patted her hand and put his arm over the back of the sofa. His fingers brushed Mori's shoulder. He thrilled to the touch and hoped she felt the same way.

"Frank was here yesterday, while you were away."

"Yes, I know."

"The men from the fire department think a cigarette may have started the fire."

"That jerk. I told him we didn't allow smoking around the barn. But, he was here early, long before the fire started." Her voice and the rapid movements of her eyelids reflected her wrath. "I don't consider that the good news. What's next?"

"Well, it lit in horse biscuits, smoldered for hours before the wind caused it to burn." In that moment Mark decided not to relate to her Frank's announcement that the two of them were to remarry.

"Hmmm," Mori said. "Pioneer women used cow and horse chips to burn in their stoves."

"There's a rumor that Frank is in partnership with a developer who happens to be Shawna. It was hard for me to believe, but then nothing she does surprises me."

"So that's what he is up to. Well, he has some hard news coming to him." Mori clenched and unclenched her hands in irritation. Her nostrils flared angrily.

Mark felt happier than he had for many years and he laughed again.

"I don't see any reason to laugh. He burned our barn down. He'll pay for it if it's the last thing I do." The words crashed against the walls.

"Calm down, Mori."

"Calm down! I've never been so angry. That–that– that man." She bristled, her dark eyes appearing almost black.

"It'll be hard to prove his cigarette started the fire although it probably did and your insurance is going to pay for most of the loss."

"That's good news, but Frank is not going to get away with this."

Mark continued to smile, delighted to hear Mori vent her feelings against Frank. "Tom and Ann are bringing riding gear down tomorrow. They contacted some of the ranchers and managed to round up extra gear and Jake says neighbors and customers called all day. Many plan to be out tomorrow to help with the cleanup. My friend has already sent a front loader and a truck so some of the debris is being removed now. I don't think it'll take long to be ready to rebuild. We can get some contractors out here to give you bids. In the meantime, we'll move the office into Cecile's garage and Jake's putting up a leanto for the animals."

Nothing could have given Mark more joy than the sight of Mori's face. He couldn't resist squeezing her shoulder as he felt her spirit return.

"I love you, Mori," Mark blurted out the words that he had planned to reserve until they were in more romantic surroundings.

A gasp escaped Mori and her eyes widened in surprise. "Oh, Mark, do you know what you are saying?"

"I'm of sound mind." He took her face in his hands and kissed her gently. "I hope you love me."

"I do," Mori paused. "I can't believe this is happening." Mark stood and pulled Mori to her feet. She melted into his arms. He could feel her heart pounding against his chest. When he looked into her eyes, he knew nothing better could happen to him than Mori and his love for her.

"I loved once and lost. What if that happens again?" There was a hint of fear in Mori's voice.

"It won't happen again. We won't allow that." Mark ran his hand through her dark silky hair.

"But look at me, I haven't even paid my mortgage and now I have to borrow more money for the new barn."

Mark put his index finger to her lips to silence her. "I

can't think of any person I'd rather share problems with than you. Life is full of problems. I want to share everything with you, the good and the bad. We'll work this out together." His expression was full of love for her.

Mori put her arms around his waist as he pulled her close to him. He touched her ear with his lips, then her chin as he said, "I love you, Mori."